Evie's War

Rori Bleu

Rosie Chapel

Ulfire Pty Ltd

First printing: 2022
ISBN: 978-0-6454794-2-3 (ebook)
ISBN: 978-0-6454794-3-0 (paperback)

Ulfire Pty. Ltd.
P.O. Box 1481
South Perth
WA 6951
Australia

Cover Design: Rebecca Norman
Images Courtesy: Canva and Deposit Photos
Designed in Canva.

❀ Created with Vellum

Acknowledgments

Rori Bleu

Special thanks to...

Jean Forrester for helping bring the characters to life, as well as the story.

Terry Fielding for allowing me to spam her mailbox with rough drafts.

Annette Begeschke, **Jo Anne Vesledahl,** and **Sheri Meece** for being forced to continue beta reading.

Rebecca Norman for her extraordinary talent in developing the beautiful cover as well as her insistence in observing the rules of proper English.

And to my co-author, **Rosie Chapel** for knowing fancy, romantic words.

Acknowledgments
Rosie Chapel

Thank you, Rori for your incredible generosity in inviting me to be co-author for this amazing story. Clearly, my advice that we ought not collaborate fell on deaf ears!!
I am truly honoured.

Melanie Duval — for being kind enough to read the final draft — thank you. Your time and quick eye is much appreciated.

As always, special thanks to my hubby for working his technical wizardry to publish the book… he's definitely a keeper!

Authors' Note

Please note, since this book is set in 1944 France, we have tried to remain true to the period in every facet of the story.

While aware and respectful of our readers' sensibilities, certain terms, which may be considered less suitable today, were the norm in the era and, as such, authentic in this context.

Rori and Rosie

Evie's War

Chapter One

"You're a coward, Choltitz," Standartenführer Johan Kristansen accused his superior who was sitting behind the desk, busy with paperwork, the younger Nazi officer assumed was the formal surrender of the city garrison to whichever Allied Force arrived in Paris first.

Errant bullets from British Sten guns in the hands of the French Resistance shattered the windows of the room in the Hôtel Le Meurice which housed Choltitz's office, tearing holes along the ornate walls on the opposite side.

The assault silenced the bickering pair, who found themselves cowering behind the desk searching for protection from any fortunate sniper.

The sound of gunfire moved away down the rue de Rivoli. Choltitz stood up, brushed himself off and lectured his aide-de-camp, "Listen to me, Kristiansen, the war is over for us and if you had any intelligence, you would dig yourself into whatever snowbank you climbed out of in Norway, and pray no one there ever finds you."

"Bah! I should have known from the start how little faith the Prussian aristocracy has in our Führer."

"It has nothing to do with faith, you fool. I am a firm believer in self-preservation."

"And while you are saving your own hide, you blatantly refuse to execute the Führer's Das Ruinenfeld Order?"

"Tell me, Kristiansen, what purpose would be served by leaving Paris as a field of ruin?"

"It would punish the Parisians and the Allies for daring to reclaim this corrupt, cesspool of a city. You would not only be doing the Third Reich an invaluable service, but also the world as a whole."

"Wrong! It is naught but the tantrum of a madman who knows his end is near and, for me to pay heed to such lunacy, would result with my neck in a noose for war crimes. I do not think so. I, for one, would rather turn out the lights and hand back the keys to the original management."

One hand on his highly polished leather holster, Kristiansen warned, "I should shoot you where you stand for treason."

Choltitz brushed aside the threat. "Do what you think is necessary, but I assure you my guard…" he waved to a point beyond Kristiansen, "…will place a bullet neatly into the back of your skull before you can get your service pistol out of your holster."

Kristiansen glanced over his shoulder to see a blonde Oberleutnant standing behind him with his Luger levelled at Kristiansen's head.

Throwing up his hands, Kristiansen marched past the soldier, stopping at the door long enough to inform Choltitz,

"Do not think this will not go unreported to High Command."

"Ja, ja," Choltitz retorted. "If they wish to punish me, tell them to contact me in London."

Office of Generalfeldmarschall Wilhelm Keitel
Oberkommando der Wehrmacht
Wünsdorf, Brandenburg, Germany
9th September 1944

Kristiansen tried to contain his fury, while he cooled his heels in Generalfeldmarschall Keitel's outer office.

The general's orders to appear, had led to Kristiansen fighting his way out of Paris.

Upon exiting the hotel, he had discovered the German vehicles, normally available to any Gestapo officer, were being used as barricades behind which the French Resistance had stationed their snipers. His only option, to make a mad dash for the motor pool near the edge of the city.

Twice during his flight, Kristiansen was compelled to snatch up a Karabiner 98k rifle from the body of a fallen German soldier, and return fire. Fortunately for Kristiansen, his years of hunting in the Norwegian forests had trained him to be a better marksmen than the butchers, prostitutes, and postal workers who were firing at him with whatever weapon they had managed to scrounge.

The same could not be said for his third encounter.

Contrary to the drowsy policeman he expected to find keeping watch over the motor pool, he discovered it was being guarded by a heavily armed member of French Milice.

Kristiansen despised this particular group, deeming them treacherous, psychotic lapdogs of the French General, Pétain.

He knew the German generals regarded him in the same light, but to Kristiansen, his kills were necessary and justifiable, especially as he believed his Norse ancestry offered a more profound link to the ancient Aryans than even Hitler could claim.

Kristiansen confronted the guard. "I need a car posthaste."

"Non," the man replied.

"Peasant, I am SS-Standartenführer Kristiansen. I have orders from High Command to report immediately."

The militiaman threw the cigarette he was smoking onto the ground. "Monsieur, I couldn't care less whether the orders came directly from that crazy Austrian, you worship. You will not take any of these cars. I too have my orders and am responsible for ensuring all of my countrymen who believed the German lies are evacuated safely from Paris."

Lifting the barrel of the small machine gun he had strapped around his neck, he nudged the end into Kristiansen's chest. "Now, be on your way before I forget we are supposed to be allies."

This was the opportunity Kristiansen needed. Grabbing the barrel, he pushed it skyward. The metal scorched his palm as, instinctively, the guard pulled the trigger, spraying lead around them.

Grabbing his dagger from its sheath, Kristiansen thrust it into the man's chest.

The guard slumped to the ground, a dark red stain blossoming over his blue uniform jacket.

Kristiansen snatched the Frenchman's wide beret to remove the blood from the blade before replacing the knife on his belt.

Unhurriedly, he stepped over the dead man, and helped himself to a Kubelwagen staff car.

Not his first choice of vehicle, but time was of the essence.

Kristiansen travelled east along bomb-pocked roads towards the French border, the petrol running out some one hundred kilometres from Luxembourg City. From there, he had no alternative but to cover the remaining distance on foot.

Finally, he reached the city's outskirts, only to discover it offered no more respite than he had the misfortune to suffer during his escape through the French countryside.

Most of the High Command based there had already been *summoned* to Berlin for some mysterious preparatory meeting for the defence of the Rhine. With no available four-wheeled transportation, Kristiansen *appropriated* a motor-cycle to make his way to the capital where he was informed he had to report to Wünsdorf, thirty kilometres to the south.

After the inconvenience the Germany military had put him through to attend this meeting, Kristiansen did not expect to be kept waiting for three hours in a stuffy office while other officers gained immediate entrance to Keitel's inner sanctum.

Kristiansen heard various levels of muffled shouting. At one point, when, momentarily, the doors stood ajar, he swore he spied Heinrich Himmler flinging papers at a man in a camel-coloured jacket who was hunched over the table.

The latter's black hair was beginning to show signs of greying, and there appeared to be a tremor in his hand when he jabbed an accusatory finger at the challenger facing him.

The doors slammed shut before he could be certain.

Time dragged on. Kristiansen glanced at his watch. It was nearly seventeen-hundred hours. His stomach had already reminded him, he had missed lunch and now, dinner time approached. Kristiansen contemplated excusing himself to the secretary, and re-arranging this meeting to a more convenient time.

Rising from his seat, he straightened his black uniform,

and was about to clear his throat to get the officer's attention, but never got the chance.

The doors to Keitel's office swung open again. The Generalfeldmarschall glared at Kristiansen as though the Norwegian was the one who had the effrontery to be tardy for their meeting.

"Are you just going to stand there, Kristiansen? I am a busy man running a war with no time to waste on the likes of you."

"I beg your forgiveness, min General." Kristiansen's native Norwegian slipped into his apology.

Keitel stomped into his office.

Kristiansen followed, thinking contemptuously. *The higher these damn Prussians are ranked, the more pompous they become.*

Save the general, the office was empty of its previous occupants. A quick scan of the room led Kristiansen's eye to a door in the wall to his right which, he surmised was their egress.

Without offering the junior officer a chair, Keitel walked over to a pile of maps and documents strewn across a large table.

His back to Kristiansen, Keitel remarked, "Did you happen to see the Third Army on your way here?"

"No, Sir," Kristiansen replied. "But I am sure our glorious Panzers will block their advance before they risk crossing the Rhine." He parroted the propaganda gleaned while traversing the Fatherland.

Keitel scoffed, "If der Führer's ingenious strategy to stop the Russians fails, we can only pray the Americans beat them to Berlin."

"What was that, Generalfeldmarschall?"

"You are aware that your former superior officer paraded

himself through Paris alongside Leclerc and Soustelle as though he was some French General liberating the city?"

Kristiansen remained silent. To add further information was redundant. Gestapo Intelligence had already beaten him to the punch.

Keitel picked up a sealed envelope from his desk and handed it to the Norwegian.

The envelope bore Adolf Hitler's personal seal.

"You will deliver these orders to der Führer's battalion tank commander, Oberst Friedrich König. You will find him in Hanover. Once you meet up with him, the two of you will make arrangements to carry out the instructions enclosed."

"May I inquire as to what these orders entail?"

"You will know soon enough, Kristiansen. I expect you to be there by noon tomorrow."

"Might I be permitted to requisition a car from the motor pool?"

"What do you think this is? A holiday resort in Nice? Make do with what you arrived in."

Kristiansen gritted his teeth at the rebuke, but the motorcycle was better than walking. *If only I can remember where I left it.*

"And Kristiansen, I cannot stress enough the urgency of completing your preparations. We are about to launch an all-out assault on the enemy's lines, and you must be ready to fulfill your part."

"Ja, min General. You can depend on me."

"I heard the same thing from that traitor Choltitz."

"I assure you, whatever it is you ask of me will be carried out to perfection."

"Ja, Ja," Keitel replied, moving to his chair behind the desk. He fell silent rummaging through the documents.

Kristiansen was unsure whether he was being dismissed.

After a few moments of awkward silence, he ventured, "If there is nothing else, I will be on my way."

Clicking his heels together, he saluted. "Sieg Heil."

Keitel did not look up from his papers, but said in an ominous tone, "Success or failure, Kristiansen, I never want to see your face again."

Kristiansen thought about giving the German a derogatory Norwegian retort about hiding under his mother's skirts, but figured it would be lost on the man.

Instead, he walked out and shut the door.

Scarcely registering Kristiansen's departure, Keitel continued to read the order he was handed by Himmler before the latter left his office. There were no fancy code names for this document. Its heading was straightforward.

Plan for Smuggling Hitler out of Germany.

The first couple of lines summed up the entire reason for the plan:

The war is all but lost. It is imperative we do not allow the Führer to fall into enemy hands... especially those of the Bolsheviks.

Chapter Two

Café la Fête
Paris, France
2nd December 1944
11:32 PM

Genevieve Rousseau glanced at the clock for the umpteenth time in the last five minutes, growing impatient waiting for the American captain to put in an appearance.

It wasn't the first time he had been either late or had stood her up altogether, but he always offered some lame excuse, which made her laugh and forgive him.

More important than the night they would spend drinking cheap Vichy wine and sharing her bed, was the information he was good for. Genevieve felt bad using him this way, but the French Resistance wanted to be part of the final victory over the Germans and the damn Americans weren't exactly forthcoming with their latest strategy.

So much for being our trusted allies, she grumbled to herself.

Genevieve took another sip of wine as she waited.

If he does not show by midnight...

She hesitated to finish the thought, realising there was a decent likelihood of being arrested for contravening the Americans' newly imposed curfew on the city of Paris.

When Paris was under German control, an arrest for violating the law would lead to hours, even days, of beatings and interrogations at the hands of the Gestapo. The black suits believed anyone out past dark held ill intent against der Führer and his benevolent Reich.

As for the Americans' time edict, none had yet learned its consequences, but de Gaulle, himself, had ordered all the resistance cells to respect the *request* of the Allied High Command.

"They, too, have shed blood in the liberation of the city and are only interested in the preservation of peace for Paris," de Gaulle had added to the cable outlining his decree.

In the end, not much had changed in Paris since management switched hands from the Germans to the Americans.

Sure, they said de Gaulle and his Provincial Government were in charge, but it was only with the blessing of the Allied overlords and their weapons.

Invariably, Genevieve's disappointment with matters of state resulted in the same remorseful sigh, "If only Claude had survived Calais."

Regrettably, his generals had thrown him and his unit to the wolves in order to stall the Germans long enough for the British to abandon the French at Dunkirk.

She swore, if her heroic Claude had escaped, he would have taken control of the Free French Forces of the Interior (FFI) and led them to an early and decisive victory over the German dogs.

Lifting her glass to her lips, she muttered to the wine, "He definitely would not have sat on his ample derrière in Algiers, like de Gaulle, and played general, while brave men went to their deaths in his name. Claude would have been in the thick of the battle."

Genevieve blinked back tears as she thought of her martyred husband. Bravely, he and his men had repelled the onslaught to the last shell. The Allies murdered him as much as had the Axis forces.

His death was the driving factor behind her decision to join the FFI in the first place. She couldn't sit by and let the collaborators, now in charge of the Vichy government, betray her country.

Genevieve had fulfilled every task her handlers asked of her. Whether it was acting as a courier, or assisting in planting bombs to destroy transports of German soldiers, or the other things. Things she would neither discuss with another living soul, nor be able to erase from her memory.

It made her retch to think of what she had done to obtain vital information. No amount of French wine could ever wash the taste of stale German beer from her mouth, especially when she had been obliged to kiss it from some Gestapo officer's lips.

War drives good people to do bad things.

That simple mantra made it easier for Genevieve to justify her actions.

In the, not quite, four months since the Allies deigned to liberate Paris, she had continued to defend herself against accusations she was a *horizontal* collaborator. There had been demands to shave her glossy tresses, as they had already done to countless women who endured sleeping with the enemy to survive.

Fortunately, she had enough important friends in the FFI to protect her... and who were indebted to her. She may never receive a medal from de Gaulle for her sacrifices, but Genevieve would be damned before she let any bastard lay a hand on her hair.

Glancing up at the clock once more: 11:49. "Putain d'enfer," she grouched under her breath. "Where are you?"

She could see the waitstaff giving her the hairy eye as they decided amongst themselves who would be the one to kick her out. The Americans loved to complain about how rude French waiters were to them but, in truth, they were asses to everybody.

Returning her attention to her wine and the door, the days before the American tanks swarmed into Paris came to mind.

Word had reached the Resistance that the Germans were about to send a final train out of the city filled with political prisoners, including captured Allied airmen, to the Dachau concentration camp. A decision had been reached that now was the time to take a direct stand.

The uprising began in the guise of a strike started by the employees of the Paris Metro, the Gendarmerie police force, and the Sûreté.

The final trigger which detonated the powder keg was the brutal attack on the young FFI guard at the Grande Cascade.

Exacerbated when the Resistance discovered that Hitler, acting like a spoiled child, had demanded the complete destruction of the city.

If he couldn't have Paris, nobody could.

The chairman of the municipal council had begged the German military governor not to follow Hitler's orders to level the city.

By now, the wine had unhinged her tongue... and her anger against all men.

To the staff, she growled, "How can any Parisian hail Choltitz as the *Saviour of Paris...*"

The very utterance of that phrase left a disgusting taste in Genevieve's mouth... slightly less than a certain male body part… but not by much. Wanting to rid herself of it, she spat on the floor.

"…for doing something any sane person, with a grain of civility, would have done. To hell with the twenty-five hundred Resistance fighters who lay dead or injured in the streets because he refused to hand over the city, leaving us no choice but to take it by force.

"To hell with you all."

Her jumble of thoughts was interrupted by the sudden appearance of the waiter. She had sensed him there before she heard him speak.

"Madame, it is late and we must close," he tried, gently, to prod her into leaving.

"Save your breath. I'm going." She tossed her money onto the table.

Rising from her chair, Genevieve headed to the door and the cold Paris night.

No sooner had the lock clicked on the door behind her, when she was hailed from the shadows by distinctly American voice.

"Madame Rousseau."

Unobtrusively, Genevieve reached for the Walther PPK pistol, secreted in her coat pocket. It served not only as her personal protection, but was also a souvenir from the last German officer who had refused to take *non* for an answer.

"Easy," the American said, stepping into the light. "I come in peace."

He wore an officer's uniform of the US Army.

Genevieve could see the golden oak leaf on his collar, ranking him as a major. Even with that information, she kept her hand where it was, fingers around the pistol grip.

"State your business, and make it quick. It is late and I would prefer not to be arrested for violating curfew because of you," she snapped.

"Then I'm guessing you don't want to be arrested for espionage against the United States Military?" he asked, casually lighting a cigarette as he did.

A smile curled around its butt when he saw his words had silenced her temporarily. Taking the cigarette from between his lips, he offered it to her.

The major's question made her consider declining it.

Normally, Genevieve did not smoke. She hated the bitter flavour and, more so, made her long for Claude's kiss. He had never been able to break the habit, and she had loved him enough to overlook his one foible.

It occurred to Genevieve that this might well be her penultimate cigarette. The last being accompanied by a blindfold.

With studied nonchalance, she accepted the smouldering cigarette, and took a quick drag. The urge to cough hit her, instantly.

Swallowing it back, she clicked her tongue, saying, "These cheap American smokes are no match for a good Turkish blend. Only thing these are good for is to get some German woman in bed."

The major chuckled. "I'm sure the American Tobacco Industry will approve of your rousing opinion, Madame Rousseau. I bet they use it in their next campaign."

Inhaling the unfiltered cigarette more deeply, ignoring the acrid burning sensation at the back of her throat, she handed it back with a demure smile.

In her sweetest voice she replied innocently, "General..." Genevieve was well-versed in stroking men's egos. Inflating an American G.I.'s rank was always a good start. "...please forgive me but I am not familiar with this Madame Rousseau to whom you keep referring.

"My name is Noelle Dufort..." Genevieve let the pistol slip from her grasp as she withdrew her hand from her pocket to rifle through her bag as though searching for papers to prove her identity. "I work as a waitress here at Café la Fête. I am trying to get home before the cur—"

Drawing another puff of the cigarette, the major sighed as he exhaled. "Madame Rousseau, it's late and cold, and insulting my intelligence isn't helping your cause. You came here tonight to meet Captain Levit. Nice guy, turned on you like a rabid dog when I found maps of the upcoming incursions into the Fatherland in his possession."

Genevieve blanched. There was no denying she was screwed.

Looking around, she tried to find a quick escape, but the American read her mind.

"Please, don't try, Madame Rousseau. I hate running in these shoes, and shooting you would be such a waste."

Her attempt to retrieve her gun was thwarted when the major, delicately but firmly, caught her by the wrist.

Taking advantage of Genevieve's struggle to break free, he dug the weapon out of her pocket, levelling it at her as he relaxed his grip.

Flexing her hand, she took a defiant step towards him. "You would shoot a decorated member of the Free French Forces — in the middle of Paris, no less?"

"Decorated? Nah," he countered sarcastically. "Overpainted might be a better description."

The slur earned him a sharp slap across his left cheek.

Rubbing his face, the major smiled and went on. "As for shooting a member of the French Resistance, yeah I'd probably get reprimanded for that. However, ridding France of a recognised collaborator and, perhaps, a suspected German spy... I'm sure de Gaulle would forgive me. Hell, he might even give me *your* medal."

Even as she balled her slender hand into a fist, preparing to make him pay for his insolence, she questioned him.

"Am I under arrest, Major...?" She dragged out his rank in the hope he would take the hint and divulge the name he had neglected to provide, so adroitly, throughout this exasperating exchange.

"Oh, how rude of me. Major Jackson Donovan, Third Army." Donovan tipped his cap.

"What is that colourful word you Americans like to use, Major? Bullshit? I can identify US Army Intelligence as easily as I can recognise the Gestapo."

"Feel free to call me Jack, Genevieve... I hope you don't mind if I use your given name."

"I'm tired, *Major Donovan*, either arrest me or tell me what the hell you want."

"Perhaps a cup of coffee and ten minutes of your time."

"Does that mean you will return my pistol, if I say *Oui*?"

"Only if you promise not to shoot me with it."

Genevieve fell silent for a moment, before saying, "Fine, I will take you up on the coffee."

Donovan cocked his head, awaiting her reassurance with regard to the gun. Receiving none, he pressed, "And the part about not shooting me?"

"I have yet to decide."

Tucking the weapon into his pocket, he patted it through his uniform coat. "In that case, Madame Rousseau, we'll leave it here for safe keeping."

Stepping to the car at the curb, he opened the passenger door to his commandeered black, two-door Peugeot 402 Eclipse, inviting her to take a seat, "Shall we?"

"Do you not think this a trifle garish for an American intelligence operative?"

Donovon shrugged. "If it was good enough for Hauptscharführer Misselwitz's mistress—"

"I should have garrotted the bastard when I had the

chance. Or better yet, tortured him as mercilessly as he did my compatriots."

Shutting the door behind her, Donovon leaned on the open window to remark drily, "I guess that explains why I had to save this poor girl from the pitchfork and torch brigade. Seems they were preparing to wreak senseless vengeance on her."

Chapter Three

Hôtel Le Meurice
Jack Donovan's Suite
Office of Strategic Services (OSS)
3rd December 1944
12:15 AM

Donovon strove to dazzle Genevieve with his military exploits as the two motored their way through the dark and empty streets of Paris.

"If I do say so myself, it was pretty harrowing landing behind the German lines in the run up to the Normandy invasion."

Glancing at his silent companion, he flashed her a smile. "Can you believe the brass would send me and a couple of greenhorn pilots up to try to hide in the midst of a hundred bombers from the Ninth Air Corp?"

His story failed to pique Genevieve's interest.

Undeterred, Donovon rambled on, "How ludicrous, you say? I know, I thought somebody at HQ had lost their mind when I heard the details. Our puny transport plane was nearly sandwiched more than a few times between those B-24s.

"Anyway, as I was about to say, it surprised me that the crate of automatic rifles I was delivering parachuted safely outside of Caen.

"Can't say the same thing for the transport. No sooner had I jumped from the rear door after the crate, than flack hit the plane and blew it out of the sky. Never did hear whether those guys made it or not. Casualties of war and all I guess.

"I'm just grateful we were able to deliver the weapons. I'd hate to think what would have happened to the FFI if we hadn't armed you in time for the push into Normandy. From what I hear, the General Staff were impressed with the roles you all played."

Genevieve let him prattle on, paying scant attention to his tale....

...she had dealt with his type before. They showed up offering promises and reassurances of help and support. But, as soon as the firing started, they all disappeared. She had no doubt, Major Jack Donovan was cut from the same cloth...

...until he mentioned the automatic weapons the Allied High Command had him accompany. That prompted a raised eyebrow and a... "That was you? Dear Lord, how did I not recognise the legendary American who endangered his life to liberate my country?"

She paused briefly to let her sarcasm sink in. "And were you referring to those American antique rifles from the last *War to End All Wars*? If so... did you forget to include their firing pins, deliberately?"

"What? That's impossible," Donovon tried refute, at which Genevieve curled a contemptuous lip.

"Seems there was a small oversight in England when they were being prepared to ship. Even though they did look imposing, only about half of them actually worked. Unfortunately, for those brave men who depended on them when they took on the German rearguard, saying *Bang, Bang* brought neither success on the battlefield, nor any hope of returning home afterwards.

"Your heroism left the resistance with one question. Did Allied High Command forget to have the rifles inspected by accident... or did they send us defective weapons with the sole purpose of using us as cannon fodder?

"If it was the latter, I would be upset, if I were you. It appears somebody in England has an axe to grind with you as well... sending you on a frivolous mission to babysit useless guns."

The major, who found himself speechless after Genevieve's all too credible observation, began a mental check through the list of suspects back in Portsmouth.

When the Peugeot turned onto rue de Rivoli, and cruised to a standstill at the entrance of the Hôtel Le Meurice, Genevieve shook her head in disbelief.

After the Germans had paraded down the Champs Élysées, in front of weeping crowds of Parisians, High Command pressed the grand hotel into service as the headquarters for General Dietrich von Choltitz's military government.

Currently, it served as Les Grandes Asperges', aka General Charles de Gaulle, temporary seat of power.

As though it wasn't insulting enough to French pride that the damned Germans had sequestered this grand hotel to perpetuate their oppression? she thought to herself. *Now, this arrogant OSS officer has taken up residence here, as well. Right under de Gaulle's humongous beak, no less.*

The opening of her door interrupted her contempt. Genevieve looked up to see Major Donovan extend his hand to her. His expression appeared to be one of genuine chivalry.

Wordlessly, he waited for her to accept.

She was taken aback by the gesture, especially bearing in mind how rude she had been.

I have spent the last quarter of an hour ignoring or denigrating this man, and still he has it within him to behave like a gentleman.

It was years since anyone had thought to do something so menial, yet meaningful, for Genevieve. The last man had been her husband, Claude, the night he took her to dinner and the cinema before leaving to report to Calais.

The simple act weakened her resolve for hatred... marginally... not only for the situation she found herself in, but also for the man who offered his hand so graciously.

Not disposed to let the major know she was touched by his gallantry... persuading herself it had to be part of his training, she hardened her gaze. Refusing to take his hand, she slid out of the car and smoothed her skirt. "Can we hurry this along, Major Donovan?"

Nodding, he shut the car door and escorted her into the lobby of the Meurice.

Leaving Genevieve in an overstuffed chair in the middle of the once decorative marble... worn by the abuse of its former occupiers... Donovon strolled over to the clerk manning the reception desk.

Genevieve watched the interaction between the two men. She was not sure, but it sounded as though the American was conversing in passably fluent French. He picked up what looked like a set of files from the counter and said, "Bonne nuit, François."

Rejoining his guest, Donovon remarked, "Nice guy, François... for MI-6."

Glancing at the clerk, Genevieve could not believe she had mistaken the man as a native of her country.

As the two entered the lift, she quizzed, "Precisely, how many countries have spies in Paris?"

Pressing the button for the top floor, he shrugged. "Not sure, I lost count with the Swedes."

The silence which met them when Jack opened the grill was more unnerving to Genevieve than the one which had hung over them on the ride up.

Ushered along the corridor, she noticed some of the doors were riddled with bullet holes.

Others had been taken off their hinges, revealing the inner rooms, their windows boarded up, awaiting replacement glass. Lingering evidence of the fierce battle which had taken place in the heart of Paris.

Reaching the only door which was oddly untouched, Donovon unlocked the deadbolt.

He opened the door and flipped on the light, illuminating a room cluttered with maps and documents.

Unsure whether he had been granted the privilege to address Genevieve by her first name, Donovan reverted to appropriate etiquette and, gathering up a pile of papers from one of the red velvet-cushioned chairs, invited, "Please have a seat, Madame Rousseau. Let me fetch you that cup of coffee."

"I'm fine, Major Donovan. What is it you want of me — besides finding you a maid to organise this mess?" she said, scanning the room.

"Maybe I'll have that luxury, if I ever get back to Washington." He grinned. "Come now... why spoil such an elegant filing system, especially given my briefcase doubles as a safe. No, all a maid would be is superfluous."

"Superfluous? That is a big word for an American... and used correctly in a sentence no less. I am impressed."

"Well, I do the Times Crosswords whenever my mail catches up to me. Taught me a word or two to charm French women."

They shared a cynical chuckle.

"So, Madame Rousseau..." Donovan continued.

"Major Donovan, social formalities were a casualty of this cursed war years ago. Just call me Evie," Genevieve invited with the merest hint of a smile.

"Then please, Evie, my name is Jack. Though, I hope it sounds less annoying than when you address me as Major Donovan."

"Well, Major... err... Jack, do you blame me? When your armies swept into Paris, they were just another band of marauders set on conquest.

"Worse yet, you rub it in our faces with a celebratory parade down the Champs Élysées from the Arc de Triomphe. Only difference between what Eisenhower did and what Hitler did in 1940 was that Hitler only managed to march his troops three abreast instead of twenty-four. Even you have to admit that was a little gaudy."

"Everybody has to play for the press, Evie, you know how propaganda works." Donovan's defence of his country's actions was half-hearted at best.

"Very true. It was considerate, if not photo-worthy, of your generals to grant Leclerc the honour of rolling his tanks into the city first." Evie retorted.

Donovan remained silent. He knew of allegations pertaining to the desire of the Second French Armoured Division to engage in battle which would only inflame the situation if revealed.

He hedged, "Let's just leave the grand plans to the upper brass. The two of us have more important things to discuss."

"Such as?"

"The proper utilisation of the FFI. We both know de Gaulle wants to disband the Resistance and meld the men into the *new* French Army."

"Oui," Evie sighed. "We have received word from our superiors that our days are numbered."

"And I can only assume your meetings with the former Captain Levit was your way of proving to them your continued worth."

Donovan saw the twinge of sadness which clouded her face at his description. He couldn't help but sympathise with this talented woman. They both were seeing the possible end of her military career.

"So you are about to — how do you Americans put it — extort information from me? I'd rather die than betray my country!"

Donovan walked over to a table covered in papers, searching for the right one. Her accusation almost caused him to laugh as he unfurled the battle map he had liberated from Levit.

"Quite the contrary, Evie, I need the expertise of you and your men to prevent the pending invasion into Germany from bogging down into a defeat in French snow."

Hesitant at first, eventually, she joined him at the table. Captain Levit had been true to his word on the importance of the map.

It showed the current positions of Allied advances, as well as a buildup of the German Group B Army and six Panzer tank divisions of the Oberkommando der Wehrmacht.

She traced the lines with the tip of her finger, taking in all of the information the map was giving. Looking up at Donovan, she said in subdued tones, "This is the final battle for France isn't it?"

Donovan nodded, his eyes taking in her soft blue gaze for the first time this evening, "Yes, Evie, and perhaps the war. I need you and your unit to see it doesn't end in an Allied defeat."

"If your High Command has this all planned out, what good will we do?"

Chapter Four

Major Donovon dropped two thick, dark green folders under Evie's curious eyes. Each was stamped *Top Secret: Authorized Personnel Only*.

Intrigued, Genevieve resisted the temptation to snatch up both to read the information Donovon was willing to share. It occurred to her, he might be setting some convoluted trap in which to snare her.

Seeing her unwillingness to touch them, Donovon opened the files and spread them out.

"Are you Authorized Personnel?" Evie joked half-heartedly.

Donovon's silence did little to alleviate her concerns, but her training as an information gatherer overrode her qualms.

Clipped to the first page of each folder was a photograph.

The first was identified as Oberst Friedrich König.

A cursory glance at the colonel's file listed him a tank commander during the First World War.

König was born in 1893 in Johannisburg, Prussia, where he also spent his early childhood.

Like his father, who had served under Otto von Bismarck

during the Franco-Prussian War, in 1911, the young König was sent to the Prussian War Academy to fulfill his duty to his state and family, and straighten himself out.

His school records did not shower him in glory. His ability to lead others, either in the field or... and more often... in a fight at some biergarten, his saving grace from expulsion.

There was nothing noteworthy about the man's military service from 1915 — when he volunteered for the Imperial German Army — until 1918, when he emerged from obscurity.

In March of that year, an engagement between the British and the Germans, saw the first successfully developed tanks enter the battlefield... the German A7V. Led by König, the A7V's plowed through the smoke laden *No Man's* land and into the British lines. The King's men were no match for the behemoths, triggering a chaotic retreat.

König's next encounter was the first true tank-on-tank confrontation with the newer British Mark IV's at the battle of Villers-Bretonneux.

Before his tank was set ablaze by a direct British strike, König had destroyed two of the enemy's vehicles outright and disabled a third.

It was also noted that he was severely burned in the incident, sidelining him for the remainder of the war.

While he recuperated in a German hospital, König's efforts were recognised by Kaiser Wilhelm II who presented him with the Iron Cross First Class and the Wound Medal.

After the War, he was awarded the coveted Tank Battle Badge, of which only a hundred were ever issued.

There was nothing on the man after 1921 except a footnote someone had scribbled claiming Oberst Friedrich König had been slain during Hitler's Munich Beer Hall Putsch in 1923.

Looking up from the file, Evie asked, "Why would the Allies care about some dead tanker? It says here he died between the wars."

"Keep reading, Evie, and I'll brew us some coffee."

Unsure of what else she could find in the documentation, she did as Donovon suggested.

Flipping through the pages towards the end of the dossier, it appeared that from 1923, until Hitler assumed dictatorial control of Germany in 1933, König was a virtual ghost.

Then, she found an intercepted communique dated September 14, 1936. It corresponded with Germany's intervention at the onset of the Spanish Civil War between the Second Spanish Republic and Generalissimo Francisco Franco's Fascist Nationalists, and read:

As per the Führer's orders, first consignment of FK's designed P-1s was delivered to Nationalists.

Technical and Tactics will remain in his hands to ensure satisfactory implementation.

She caught movement out of the corner of her eye, and lifted her head to see Jack offering her a steaming cup of coffee.

Accepting the drink, she asked, "Are you trying to tell me a dead man developed the German's Panzer Tank Force?"

"Not only that Evie, but he used the Spanish Civil War as a testing ground to transform the lumbering and antiquated, German shit-houses into sleek, lethal killing machines, designed specifically for the Führer's Blitzkrieg."

"But how? How did he slip from the view of every military intelligence organisation around the globe?"

"The party's high ranking officials went out of their way to exaggerate his death, while camouflaging his true activities and whereabouts. Don't forget, the Germans were not allowed to develop... let alone build... any tanks at all."

Evie took a sip of the coffee ignoring its bitter taste, before reciting out loud. "After the Spanish Civil War, the Germans went on to implement what they had learned to invade Poland in the east. From there, they overran the Low Countries in the west, on their way to their ultimate destination..." she paused, hating to say it. "...France."

Scouring the subsequent pages, she found no further mention of König. Confused, she was about to question Donovon on this man's importance, given everyone on the face of the planet was familiar with the German Blitzkrieg.

Before she could get the words out, he repeated, "Just keep going."

"Allied Command has no concrete evidence to confirm whether König is the *FK* mentioned in the communique, nor is there any record of him serving as an official member of the Heer... the German Army," she elaborated.

Jack hid a grin at Evie's clarification, deeming it unnecessary to mention that he had long been conversant with the three branches of the German military.

In the meantime Evie was reciting, "Intelligence has identified a special battalion of Tiger tanks along with its commander, being assigned to the 1st Panzer Division Leibstandarte SS. They proved themselves formidable against the Soviet's T-34s in the Russian Caucasus. Military strategists agree, had this battalion been allowed to roam unencumbered by Hitler's ineptitude, they could have captured the oilfields in Baku.

"Jealousy among the field commanders had this unit recalled to Berlin on the grounds of insubordination on its commander's part, from where they were sent to the Western Front in new Tiger IV tanks, assigned to the 503rd Heavy Panzer Battalion, and answerable only to Hitler."

She reached the last page of the dossier. "Why does any of this matter?"

"As of two days ago, a detachment of forty-five Tiger IV tanks, which were being tracked by our reconnaissance, mysteriously disappeared somewhere southeast of the Ardennes Forest."

"Please explain how you lose forty-five heavy tanks?"

"If I knew that, I would not have to have bothered you this evening."

Standing to stretch her legs, Evie replaced König's file on the table, and picked up the second.

Opening the file, she needed no introduction to this man. Had she been a cat, she would have hissed.

Donovon was intrigued by her reaction to the picture.

"Tell me, Evie, what do you know of this man that we don't?"

She left the folder on the table because she already knew too much about him, witness to his cruel form of justice on the streets of Paris.

Evie collected herself and returned to her chair. She folded her hands in her lap, took a deep breath, and began.

"SS-Standartenführer Johan Kristiansen, AKA, the Nordic Wolf."

"Yes, yes," Donovon interjected, "but why does all of Europe refer to him that way? Is he some superhuman Viking hunter?"

"Hardly... and if you would kindly keep your mouth shut and stop interrupting me, Major," she scolded, "I will enlighten you."

Donovon raised his hands in submission, though the unrepentant grin on his face said otherwise, and did as she bade. Sinking back in his chair, Donovon prepared to hang on Evie's words like a child listening to his favourite bedtime story.

"When the Germans advanced into Norway, thanks in no small part to the Swedish rail system transporting German soldiers from Finland, leaving King Haakon VII and his family no choice but to flee to England to avoid becoming puppets of Berlin…"

She spotted Donovon open his mouth to say something, and raised a finger warning him to remain quiet.

"…your boy Kristiansen was one of the first in line to register for the resurgence of Vidkun Quisling's National Gathering Party.

"To assure his place in the party, he betrayed his own father to the Gestapo as a resistance collaborator. Sadly, the unsubstantiated charge earned the old man a trip to the Victoria Terrasse. He was never able to prove his innocence and died there during the interrogation.

"The fact Kristiansen was so willing to turn on his father, reflected positively in the eyes of the German Reichskommissar for Norway, Josef Terboven. He was assigned to Quisling's personal security detail.

"It wasn't long before Quisling began to distrust Kristiansen. Convinced he was a Gestapo spy, Quisling pleaded with Terboven to demote and transfer Kristiansen to Grini Fangeleir prison camp as a guard, to rid himself of someone who could so easily send a family member to their death.

"Did you know it was Quisling, himself, who gave Kristiansen his nickname?"

Donovon shook out a match he had used to light another smoke, and replied through the cigarette clenched in his lips, "Nope. Now will you allow me to ask a question?"

"Depends, but go ahead and try."

"Why? Why was he referred to as a wolf?"

"Besides what he did to his father? I assume it had something to do with the rumours swirling throughout Oslo that Kristiansen was sniffing around the Minister's wife like a dog in heat. I guess it was Kristiansen's attempt to embarrass Quisling by making the man look like a weak, omega pack wolf who could not control his own wife, let alone a country at war with itself.

"And since Terboven hated Quisling... especially after the latter went over his head and begged Hitler to give him more power... Terboven refused to allow Quisling the privilege of killing Kristiansen.

"The best Quisling could get was to see Kristiansen transferred to Gestapo headquarters at Arkivet, to serve their Counter Intelligence-E3 Department. That is where he refined his skills as an interrogator... and a merciless psychopath.

"Eventually, Terboven realised Kristiansen was more of a threat than the resistance to the fragile stability of the German occupation in Norway. The resistance went so far as to use Kristiansen's face for recruiting purposes... infuriating Quisling all the more.

"Can you imagine a narcissistic ruler like Quisling obsessing over something as petty as not being as hated as a junior SS officer?"

Evie gave a dry chuckle at the notion.

"In the end, the Germans did not want to lose his skills, so they reassigned him from the SS E4-Scandinavian to E3-Western Europe, stationed here in Paris as the aide-de-camp to SS-Obergruppenführe Carl Oberg."

"That would be the Head of the SS and police here in Paris?"

"Oui. I cannot even begin to describe the outright torture and brutal genocide inflicted on the citizens in and around Paris.

"I will never forget the day I happened to see the bastard

murder two boys for bumping into Oberg on the street. Kristiansen said something that made Oberg chuckle and, before anyone could blink, he had shot both the boys in the head.

Evie's voice dropped, "God, they were just kids." She fought the urge to weep at the memory, but her eyes glittered with unshed tears. She tried to collect herself. "W-who does that?

"The look on his face gave me chills. He held his Luger over one of the children, and proclaimed proudly, 'Let this be a lesson to you swine. Any disrespect or deliberate assault on your racial superiors will not be tolerated.' They stationed guards within shooting distance of the bodies so no one could collect them for a decent burial."

Donovon was speechless as she broke into sobs. The rest of her account was unintelligible, save her final words, "T-They were left as fodder for the ravenous strays."

Rising from his chair, Donovon padded across the room to where Evie sat. He placed what he hoped was a comforting hand on her shoulder. "I'm sorry for making you relive that."

Clearing her throat, Evie dabbed at the corner of her eyes. With a dignified sniffle, she asked, "I understand König's importance, but beyond Kristiansen's war crimes, how does he relate to this?"

"Among the papers Intelligence discovered in Choltitz's office, were a couple of cables you would normally expect him to destroy. Stuff like the cable ordering the destruction of Paris, and an order to transfer Kristiansen to the 503rd Heavy."

"Maybe Choltitz was in a hurry to surrender to Leclerc and the Free French."

"One possibility, but it might interest you to know that Kristiansen never reported to the 503. London thinks he received plans from Berlin concerning the buildup along the border of France and Germany and the Germans' final attack to break the Allied advance.

"And that's why you are here, Evie. I need you and your group to find these two."

"And, Major Donovon, what if I decide to do as *Mon Général Asparagus* prefers," her voice steeped in sarcasm, "and fade into peaceful obscurity?"

"A million-plus men will die needlessly…" Donovon hated himself for having to finish the rest of the statement, but he had no choice. "…and the new French Republic will hold you personally responsible for their deaths."

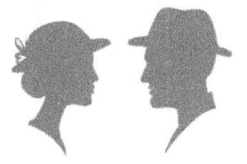

Chapter Five

32 rue de Bassano
Apartment 5
7:15 AM

P redawn had begun to colour the sky above the city by the time Donovan dropped off Evie outside her building. She had been inclined to give him a fake address, but presumed he knew where she lived and already had the residence under surveillance.

At least that's what I would do if our roles were reversed.

She sat on the front steps for a few moments, riveted, as ever, by the myriad tinges of pinks and oranges heralding the new morning as they pushed back the deep violet darkness. This was her favourite part of the day, even if it had come at the end of an exhausting night.

Grudgingly, she had helped Donovon study the classified maps for places König might hide a battalion of tanks in the Ardennes. Along with the tracking, discussions about operational strategies about what to do with the Tigers once they were found, lasted through two pots of the worst coffee she had ever managed to consume.

How the man has not poisoned himself, is anybody's guess.

"He definitely needs a woman in his life," she murmured half to herself. "I pity the poor wench."

The chill of the dawn urged her inside but before she did, and out of habit, she glanced casually up and down the street. Evie knew this district well, she had grown up playing among these streets.

She was born on the top floor of this ancient building, which had forged a young girl into the woman who now stood on its foot-worn steps, as surely as any person who might have occupied its rooms.

The memories of stories about lives lived in other parts of the world, of struggles the brave who once resided here had fought in the name of justice, and simply watching the frenzied Parisian life pass in the streets below, had imbued in her the lessons of man's humanity and cruelty.

A pang of nostalgia plucked at her heart, causing her to peek over her shoulder at the tired facade of her home.

Originally, it had belonged to her parents, and served as a bohemian boarding house from the end of the Great War. The tenants were always a motley collection of Parisians. Jazz musicians, poets, political radicals, and notable Jewish leaders had all passed through the doors at one time or another.

Fondly, the older residents — at least, those not deported by the Germans — had recounted the stories of the night Genevieve came to this world in the wee hours of the morning in her parents' bed.

It still brought a smile, albeit melancholy, to picture her father pounding on the tenants' doors to announce the joyous occasion, and of the impromptu party which, to the chagrin of her exhausted mother, began in their parlour before spilling out into the street.

Evie always suspected it was because her mother had given them the boot in order to snatch a few hours' sleep.

Threats of summoning Le Police Nationale on the raucous revellers for disturbing the peace were quickly quelled with bribes of free wine and food. Attired in night clothes, the entire neighbourhood was soon in the street celebrating.

During the Spanish Civil War, her parents opened their doors to political refugees who had fled the dictatorships of both the Fascist Franco in the south and the greater evil to the east, Adolf Hitler.

While this decision came back to haunt them, Evie knew her parents would never turn anyone away.

A person's political persuasion or religious practices should never be grounds for denying sanctuary. This was the credo on which her parents raised their daughter.

It was this steadfast belief which had brought Claude to her door.

He was a socialist demanding reform with the Third French Republic. One who had received more than his fair share of beatings at the hands of the Paris Police. Evie's father had bailed Claude out of jail with frequency.

As for Evie, she liked to sit in Claude's room, the door always open, of course, listening in fascination while he rehearsed his speeches.

Claude had proposed to, and married, Evie in the parlour. He used to say he loved the way the windows in that room seemed to glow with Heaven's light. Her husband was a hopeless romantic, even if only in private.

These same windows saw a weeping wife watch her beloved new husband wave goodbye when he was sent to

Calais. While he disagreed with his government's policies, he refused to turn his back on the storm clouds of war which threatened France.

She had wanted to accompany him to the train station, but he insisted on saying his goodbyes in their room.

Despite the circumstances, Claude was not a man to indulge in a public display of emotion. He begged her to understand. While he wanted her there, he could not bear to leave her standing alone on a station platform, like a scene from one of the poorly written romance films they had seen at the cinema. That was just his way.

It was also through these very windows that she saw the parade of grey, German Stormtrooper uniforms pass below. She had watched in disbelief as half the local residents wept, while the other half threw the infamous Nazi salute welcoming the parading invaders.

Not long after that, Evie watched from the window as her parents were strong-armed into the back of a German army truck. Some of their former neighbours had repeated whispered rumours to the Germans, implying her parents sympathised with Jews and Communists and were a threat to the stability of the new regime.

Like locusts, the Gestapo had descended on the building.

The Jewish tenants were dragooned into railcars bound for a *vacation* in Poland, along with anyone else the Military Governor judged to be suspicious and unacceptable — which included Evie's parents.

It didn't take her long to recognise what was normal on her block.

Spying an unfamiliar car parked down the curb from her door came as no surprise. She gave the occupants a friendly wave before heading in, making a mental note to take them a coffee later in the day.

She ascended the stairs to her flat, where she paused to examine her door. The scratches around the lock informed her, somebody had paid a visit during the night.

Curtly, she informed any listening device, "Presumably, the reason Major Donovan has not locked me up is because you failed to find anything. Remind me to send you the receipt for repairing my lock, Jack."

She was serious. The man was going to pay for any damage to her belongings. Opening the door, she switched on the light.

To her surprise, her flat was immaculate. Everything was in its place, which in Evie's life was a rarity. Even her post was stacked neatly on her side table.

"And yet your office is a disaster. Tsk," she laughed to herself.

Walking into the kitchen, she registered that whoever searched her home, had also tidied her cupboards.

"Maybe I should get arrested by Army Intelligence more often."

Putting a pot of coffee on the stove, she made herself comfortable while she waited for it to finish percolating.

She ran through the conversation Jack and she had earlier, pausing her recollections long enough to chastise herself for referring to the American in so cordial a manner.

The jerk had my house broken into. Non, it is back to Major Donovan with him.

Satisfied with her decision, she ruminated over how *Donovon* had ended the evening, wanting to meet with the members of her group.

Some garbage about including them in the planning. I suppose he thinks I'm gullible. It may sound like a strategic idea but, in truth, merely divulges their identities. I am sorry, Major Donovon, that does not sit well with me.

Evie contemplated contacting her cell handler, Paul, to let him know about the previous night's events. However, she was hesitant to do so.

She was sure Army Intelligence would not have gone to the trouble of searching her apartment without bothering to tap her phone, which added to her irritation, because she had just removed the Germans' listening device.

All this intrigue was an unnecessary headache, and still left her questioning whether she should reach out to Paul.

From there her mind went off on a tangent.

Was Paul even his real name? Why should I believe it is? Especially since aliases are mandatory in our line of work in case of capture.

She laughed, reminded of her own code name — Noelle. It sounded ridiculously flighty, totally lacking the cloak and dagger mystique of an alias like Marta Hari.

There is a true alias if I have ever heard one.

Though, she did feel sorry for the poor Dutch exotic dancer, the woman behind the name. The French had executed her for spying for the Germans in the last war, despite questionable evidence of her guilt. Another scapegoat? Perhaps.

The scent of the freshly brewed coffee interrupted her thoughts of international espionage and lured her into the kitchen to pour herself a cup. Unlike her associates, she drank her coffee as hot and strong as possible. She joked it helped to keep her attention focused and sharp.

Taking another sip, her thoughts drifted back to Jack's terrible offering last night. *Maybe I should teach him—*

By sheer effort of will, Evie coaxed her contrary brain away from Jack Donovan and what she might do to him, to concentrate on contacting the resistance... and Paul

Paul was a stranger's shoulder, Evie had leaned on, in a nondescript bar the night her parents were arrested. He had listened quietly while she poured her heart out over too many bottles of wine.

When he offered to see her safely home, she had half expected him to take liberties with the broken, intoxicated woman. In truth, she would not have cared had he done so... even if it meant her death followed. At that point life had no meaning.

To her surprise, although he escorted her up the stairs and to her flat, the closest he came to bedding her was when he tucked her in with a promise to check on her the following day.

Evie was startled when he knocked on her door at eight prompt, the next morning, bearing a thermos full of black coffee prepared from beans he had managed to get smuggled from Brazil through Spain and into Paris. His chivalry was evidenced further by the mouthwatering selection of fresh croissants, macaroons, and madeleines, which he had brought to accompany the coffee.

Who could resist such generosity? Not Evie. She invited him in, and they sat at her small kitchen table, savouring the pastries and coffee. Once more, Paul offered a sympathetic ear while Evie talked about life in the building before the war.

Neither mentioned the German occupation, unable to trust that the other was not a Nazi collaborator hoping to gain information on the Resistance.

Over the subsequent weeks, the two became close enough that Evie felt comfortable criticising the failure of French High Command to prevent German Panzers from barging through the Ardennes. Of how their arrogant stupidity cost the life of her husband so the French and British forces as well as the cowardly politicians in Paris, could escape capture.

At this point, Paul confronted her.

"And what do you do, Evie? Do you plan to spend the rest of your life like the rest of our countrymen, dreaming of days past while accepting our present and future complacently?

"Could you have saved your precious husband by stepping up and arming yourself? Or did you choose to hide and pray for the best?"

His words hit her like a punch to the gut.

"How dare you speak to me that way? I am a widow, what difference could I have made?"

"All the difference in the world."

"You talk arrant nonsense. Get out of my flat and do not bother to—"

Paul had no intention of leaving. He had seen the fire in her eyes when she revealed her true feelings about the war.

"Are you aware that as we speak, thousands of French both in the Occupied Zone, as well as the supposedly neutral Vichy South are being rounded up to serve as slave labor for Germany?"

Evie fell silent. She had already seen firsthand the majority of her tenants herded into those trucks destined for the rail depots and transports heading east.

"It is time for you to ask yourself, Genevieve Rousseau, are you going to allow the deaths of your husband and parents to be in vain, or are you going to join those of us still fighting to drive the Germans out of not only Paris, but France as a whole?"

That was when she knew she could not turn back.

How could she consider herself a French patriot if she refused to come to her country's aid as had her husband.

Her reply was simple. "Where do we begin?"

Evie recollected her haphazard training in marksmanship and explosives. It came in handy that the woman who lived on the second floor of the building had fled Munich when Hitler assumed control. She taught the young Evie, German so she had somebody with whom to partake of tea and conversation.

Her first mission was to play scout while her cell destroyed locomotives bound for Poland. It was during this action when she was compelled to take her first life after a guard stumbled upon her.

With no legitimate excuse for being in the rail yard, it became a matter of her life or his.

Recalling that incident led to memories of the first time she had needed to bed a German officer.

Paul had never given her overt instructions to sleep with the man. She had done so of her own accord, in order to retrieve information on the German High Command's decisions to reduce the Vichy government's so-called independence, making them a true puppet state. In fact, so against it had he been, he urged her to leave the Resistance for the sake of her humanity.

His plea fell on deaf ears. The best he could extract was a promise he could be in the next room in case things went awry.

But in the end that was all ancient history. She had new problems now.

Thanks to her earlier visitors, use of her own phone was out of the question, but what about one of her few remaining tenants' phones?

That led to another concern. If the OSS had tapped her phone, what stopped them from doing the same to every phone in the building?

She could not compromise anyone else's safety.

That option was out.

What about the payphone at the cafe down the street? She had used that on occasion during the occupation, despite her suspicion it was monitored as well. The Germans had no idea she was a member of the French Resistance, so there would be no advantage for them to have her followed, save the fact they had murdered her parents.

The same did not apply to the Americans. That bastard of an army captain, Levit, had handed her to them on a plate to protect his own ass, and she now had people watching her every move.

Evie brooded over that. Was using her own phone the worst course of action?

She didn't know where in Paris the phone on the other end of the line was ringing, then again, neither did the OSS.

And Evie did have one trick left up her sleeve.

In dire emergencies, she had been instructed to dial a number, and let it ring once. Then, after waiting for two hours, take the Metro to Pyrénées Station on Line 11.

From there, Evie should walk to the Parc des Buttes-Chaumont and find a bench in the middle of the park, whereupon she would receive further instructions.

She remembered why she had never bothered with French Intelligence. It took too long for anybody to make a move.

Sighing, she topped up her cup, took a long sip, and walked over to the table where her phone sat.

Picking up the receiver, she heard the faintest of clicks echo on the line. Dialling the number she had been told to memorise, she waited in silence. It felt like an eternity for the line to connect.

Suddenly, the receiver on the other end sprang to life with a loud ring. Evie hung up immediately.

She hoped somebody had heard it. Looking at her watch, she started the mental timer for her departure.

Chapter Six

Peeking through her blackout curtains, Evie saw one of the men, dressed similarly to Donovon, perched on the fender of the Renault, lighting a cigarette. Neither he nor his passenger made any move towards her door.

The most ominous gesture he made was to turn up the collar of his coat against the frigid morning.

Retreating, Evie knew she faced a bigger problem. She required a foolproof method to escape her flat without her American friends noticing.

One last glimpse through the curtains tugged at her ingrained sense of courtesy.

Trained by her mother to be a gracious hostess at all times, she experienced a twinge of regret that the men in the car would have to forgo her tacitly promised coffee for the time being. She *did* vow to return with some baguettes by way of apology for outwitting them.

Never in her life had Evie wasted so much time in her old, cedar armoire trying to find just the right clothes to wear. She chose something, which she hung from her mirror, stepped back to study it while sipping her coffee, then tossed the garment on her bed.

Everything was either too stylish, or too sexy, or she just outright hated them. She made sure to remember which ones would end up on the bonfire when this was all done.

A glance at the clock on the wall informed her she no longer had the luxury of dallying.

"Gah," she fretted out loud. "This was always so easy with the Germans. They expected all French women to dress like whores and act in the same manner."

But she was dealing with the OSS and Jack Donovan now.

Does he see me the same way? Nothing more than a whore who's been trained to kill and destroy? Or can he see me for who I really am?

She cursed to herself for letting the American get into her head.

Yes, he was handsome in that uncouth American way. However, Evie, she reminded herself, *he is as untrustworthy as the Gestapo, wanting you to betray your people's identities.*

Setting down her coffee, Evie rifled through her cupboard again. At the back, she came across an outfit she had forgotten about. It belonged to her mother.

It was a simple tan suit with a plain cream blouse. She remembered how dreadful her mother had looked in it. While the cut was chic, the drab colour did not flatter her mother's complexion.

Her father had purchased the outfit as a surprise, and her mother, *bless her*, had not the heart to exchange it. Her husband's look of pride when he presented his carefully chosen gift, made it impossible.

God, how I miss them, she thought, wiping away a nostalgic tear.

Holding it against her, Evie remembered her mother had been a good two sizes larger than she. The solution was so obvious it made her laugh.

"With some extra padding here and there, I could walk right past that damn car and the fools would never notice."

Hanging the suit on the back of her bedroom door, she returned to the armoire taking the chair from her dressing table with her, which she climbed on to retrieve her mother's boxes from the top of the wardrobe.

The fact they were still there represented a silent testament to Evie's fading belief that her parents would be released one day. Despite knowing, in her heart of hearts, she would never see them again, she could not bring herself to throw out the boxes.

Digging through, she found what she was searching for. Playing dress up with her mother's clothes came to mind as she looked over the beige brassiere and girdle.

"Dear Mother, if only you'd discovered colour." She smiled, happy memories suffusing her.

After depleting her father's box of socks, she stood in front of the floor-length mirror, fluffing herself. Not until the reflection of her mother smiled back at her was Evie satisfied with her appearance.

She blew a kiss to the image. "Bénis ton âme, mère," praying the Lord truly had blessed her mother's soul.

Smoothing non-existent lint off the suit, Evie took a final look in the mirror. She knew there were those in her organisation who thought she was overcautious at times.

Be that as it may, I would rather look like a frumpy, middle-aged spinster walking down a Paris path than a member of the French Resistance trying to avoid arrest.

It was something she had learned during the four years of German occupation.

Grabbing her empty mug, she returned it to the kitchen. With step one of her plan completed, it was time for step two. This would require her to enact an even more important lesson the war had taught her... *make do with what you have.*

The brown, low-heeled Oxford shoes Evie slipped her feet into, highlighted the dowdy ensemble she had been working hard to achieve, not to mention they were the most comfortable pair she owned... a happy bonus.

Retrieving her mother's cloche hat from its place of honour by the front door, she locked her apartment, then scanned the hall before heading to the attic ladder.

Before ascending, a glance over her shoulder reassured her she was alone. Pulling on the dangling rope affixed to the latch, the ladder unfolded allowing her to scamper up into the musty darkness.

Tugging the hatch shut, Evie lit the candle her father had left on a holder situated in the rafter above. Allowing her eyes to adjust to the gloom, she peered around the attic in search of the small door to the roof.

As a child, Evie used to cheat when playing hide and seek with the local children. She had often climbed up here, to scurry across the roof and jump the narrow gap to the adjacent residence.

Once on the other roof, it was an easy matter to pop open the broken door which led to the lower floors, then run down the stairs and out through the door to freedom.

Her father lectured her whenever he caught her. "One day, Evie..." he scolded, "if it does not one day lead to your death, it will surely lead to mine!"

He always worried so much about my safety.

She giggled softly, "You better come catch me, Papa."

Blowing out the candle, she exited onto the roof. Hidden from view behind the chimneys, Evie scrutinised the alley far below, not sure who might be watching the rear of the house. Traffic appeared to be heavier than usual, which was unsettling, although she did not spot anything out of place.

When she reached the ledge, Evie questioned the wisdom of her decision. The one-and-a-half-metre gap, she had once cleared without thought, appeared wider than usual. The extra weight from the padding she had stuffed into her mother's clothing, adding to her trepidation.

Right at this moment, jumping across the Seine was a more attractive proposition.

"I can do this," she commanded her anxious nerves.

Unwilling to risk a broken ankle... or worse... she removed her shoes and threw them over. Each one skidded along the opposite roof when they landed.

"Great," she lamented, "it is icy too."

Shaking off her indecision, Evie charged to the edge and jumped. The landing on the other roof was anything but graceful.

Her feet went out from under her, bringing her down on her butt with a thud.

Luckily, she avoided smacking her head against the building's brick cornice by a hair's breadth. While the extra padding helped cushion the blow, it did not ease the humiliation of her awkward touchdown.

"Putain de merde!" Evie hissed as she brushed herself off, surveying her surrounds to ensure no one had witnessed her ignominious tumble... she had her reputation to consider after all.

Putting on her shoes, she squeezed through the doorway to the interior of the residence and descended to the entrance.

Evie paused at the door, checking to see whether her

chaperones were still parked along the street. Satisfied, she angled her hat until it shaded her eyes, and headed down the steps.

Keeping her ears pricked, she prepared herself for either the approach of the government car, or the clatter of military boots giving chase.

Taking care not to look back, she walked in the opposite direction, trying to mimic her mother's matronly gait.

When she reached the small bakery not far from the apartments, Evie lingered a moment to gaze at the delicious morsels on display, using the window to make sure she was still on her own. She gave the baker a smile and wave, before turning to flag down a cab to drive her to the Metro.

Parc des Buttes-Chaumont

Evie followed the instructions to the letter.

The trek required her to pass through seven stations along Line 11 until she reached Pyrénées. From there, she strolled along the Avenue Simon Bolivar to the park, and although only a short distance, she seized the opportunity to look in every shop window she passed to reassure herself she was not being followed.

Once in the park, Evie took the path leading to Belvedere Island. Crossing the Pont des Suicidés onto the island, she quickened her pace to the Temple of Sibyl.

She made herself comfortable on a bench facing the crumbling monument, amazed it had survived the ravages of the last hundred years.

Before long, she was preoccupied by the events of the previous twelve hours, only to be startled when she felt a heavy pressure on her shoulder from an unseen source.

In her peripheral vision she saw a large hand protruding from the slightly frayed cuff of a dark brown, tweed suit coat sleeve. Its material and cut spoke of a well-traveled pre-war suit.

It does not appear to be a French style... perhaps British? Evie mused, absently.

While Paul's grip is firm, his hand is neither this large nor this unkempt.

Without turning, she threatened, "Unless you wish to have me trim your fingernails at your wrist, monsieur, I suggest you remove your hand from my shoulder this instant."

The American accented reply made her wince.

"And here I thought we had moved beyond hostilities last night, Genevieve."

Jack lifted what felt like a bear paw, and rounded the bench, to tower over Evie who, for some bizarre reason, half-expected to see him sporting a gauche beret, to blend in with the few Parisians wandering about the park.

To her relief... and amazement... Jack was wearing a tasteful fedora which matched his tailored, if slightly rumpled, suit.

Sitting next to her, Jack tucked her arm through his as though they were lovers indulging in a clandestine rendezvous. A tactic which also prevented Evie reaching for any weapon he was sure she was concealing, while nudging her wrist against his holstered .45.

"This park is somewhat out of your way, is it not?" He patted her secured arm.

"Up until a few moments ago, I was enjoying the idyllic scenery it offers, or is that a violation of some new American law?" she retorted.

"Not today, but profiteering from the war is."

Evie tried to tug her arm free. Not so much to escape

from the American, but to face him. Unsuccessful, the best she could manage was, "Have you lost your mind, Major? I have never done such a—"

"Oh, I believe you, Evie." Jack interrupted in a silky voice.

A chill rippled down her spine at his tone.

"Can you say the same thing about the guy you were waiting for? Although I suspect it's his lover's head, de Gaulle wants. Either way, both men are in front of the general this morning facing charges of profiteering and collaboration."

"You are lying, Donovan," she snapped. "I can assure you Paul would never do such a thing. As for anyone he was involved with..." Her words died off when the enormity of what Jack had just said hit her.

Evie had never questioned Paul about his personal life, it was none of her business. However, finding out his lover was a man brought a new perspective to *her* relationship with him.

The need to defend Paul ran deep, "S-surely you are mistaken, Major. There is no possible way it is Paul."

His eyes on the monument Jack said, "It doesn't really matter to me what you believe is true about your associate. I have more important issues confronting me.

"As do you, Madame Rousseau. You can either stop playing these childish spy games and accompany me to de Gaulle's office to save the two of them or you can continue to sit here and let them go to the gallows. It's your call."

Evie felt his grip loosen. She glowered at him sullenly. "It appears, I have little choice, but why do you care?"

"I need the pair of you alive to have any prospect of discovering what our Norwegian friend is up to before it's too late."

They rose from the bench, and Jack extended his arm to Evie who accepted, reluctantly.

As they headed to Donovan's waiting car, curiosity got the better of her.

"How did you know I would be here?"

"You forget you're not the only spy in the game. Besides, your sly phone trick connected to a handset at the Meurice located in what was once the office of one Henri Petit. The man whose neck you're about to save."

"B-but how did *you* learn about it?" She spun, wide-eyed, to face him.

"In whose office do you suppose I'm working?"

Jack opened the door of his waiting car but prevented Evie from entering. Looking down at his hand on her arm, she lifted a confused gaze to him.

Jack entreated softly, "Promise me, Evie, no more games between us? We don't have much time to prevent whatever insanity Hitler has planned."

Chapter Seven

L oud, angry voices reverberated throughout the ground floor of the Hôtel Le Meurice. Evie could hear Paul's defence of his actions even before she and Jack reached the doorway to de Gaulle's office situated at the end of the corridor.

"Mon Général, I assure you, everything we did was in the best interests of Paris and France. Any accusations otherwise are naught but lies brought about by those seeking to save their own lives."

"*Silence,*" de Gaulle's voice rang out. "You will speak when I grant permission, and not until."

Two men, neatly dressed in Free French uniforms and armed with American M1 rifles, flanked the entrance, seemingly unfazed by the commotion taking place inside. By the size of the crowd, most with folders or other documents in hand, gathering in the hall, the sentries' sole responsibility was to prevent anyone from gaining access.

Anyone except Major Jack Donovan. The OSS officer nodded to the men as, casually, he escorted Evie into the office.

Hearing the door open unannounced, de Gaulle's beady eyes darted towards it to see who had the audacity to violate his orders. Seeing the American's smiling face, de Gaulle's expression morphed from one of admonishment to pure hatred.

The General held all the Americans in *his* city in contempt for the way their High Command had treated him during exile in Africa, but none garnered as much rancour as Donovan.

While the entire free world acknowledged de Gaulle as the rightful head of the Provisional Government of the French Republic, de Gaulle himself suspected the major was working in the background to depose him for a more moderate American puppet.

De Gaulle had decided to use these two reprobates to demonstrate to Donovan who was actually in control of France.

Directing his vitriol at his fellow countrymen, he vented, "I have heard enough of your lies. I have a stack of documents on my desk with *your lover's* name on them..." de Gaulle's distaste for homosexuality was plain to everyone in the room, "...which proves his complicity with the Germans in draining our beloved country of its natural resources..." de Gaulle jabbed an accusatory finger at Henri, "...to the suffering and detriment of your fellow citizens."

Swinging his finger to Paul, he railed, "And as for you. You willingly accepted contraband from this man for your own personal use."

"Mon Général, the contraband of which you speak was nothing more than weapons and ammunition earmarked for the Milice Française. Would you prefer, I allowed those machine guns to fall into the hands of the Vichy militia so those swine can kill more of the resistance?"

"That decision was not up to either of you." De Gaulle

rested against the side of his desk, arms folded, and his demeanour cooled. "No, Monsieur Dufort…"

Jack cocked a brow at Evie, recalling she had essayed the same alias with him the previous night. In his haste to bring her in, he had neglected to make the connection. Now, he was unsure whether it was a deliberate ruse to gauge his reaction or merely a desperate attempt to come up with a fake name.

"…to a more discerning eye, it would appear the Germans were arming your group in order to carry out their bidding. Is that not correct, Madame Rousseau?"

All attention shifted to the lone woman in the room.

A lump swelled in Evie's throat under his burning scrutiny, while he awaited her response to the accusations.

Clearing her throat, she stared down de Gaulle. Summoning up all the devotion she could offer in Paul's defence, she demurred, "Non, mon Général, Monsieur Dufort is the finest patriot France has to offer."

Seeing de Gaulle's glare, Evie amended hastily, "Of course, with the exception of yourself, mon Général." She mustered up a smile, which de Gaulle waved off arrogantly before rounding his desk to settle into his chair.

Evie ignored the slight. "I cannot speak for the integrity of Monsieur Petit but, if Paul… excuse me… Monsieur Dufort is attesting to his service and dedication to the Republic, I am confident of his innocence."

"Bah," de Gaulle rebuffed, pounding a fist on his desk. "You three are nothing but filthy, traitorous liars. You all will find yourselves on the gallows by day's end."

"General de Gaulle, if I may?" Jack interceded.

De Gaulle shot to his feet. "Major Donovan, I do not need approval from America to handle the affairs of state within a liberated France. We are a free country with the right of self-determination and just—"

Jack held his hand up to stop the general's irritating rant, thinking, *It might work on Churchill, you puffed-up asparagus, but I don't have time for your tantrum.*

Biting back the mutual dislike and distrust he and de Gaulle shared, Jack cut in. "I can assure you, your American allies hold you in the highest esteem, General de Gaulle..."

Charles de Gaulle snorted and stalked to the window facing the rue de Rivoli, determined not to give the American the satisfaction of knowing he was getting under de Gaulle's skin.

"...what my country begs, is that you use your military genius to release these three into my custody."

Hands clasped behind his back, de Gaulle scowled, "Why should you trust them anymore than I?"

"Because I need their knowledge of the men who controlled *your* city."

At this point, diplomacy was rapidly losing its benefits, and Jack could not have cared less whether his barb had stung the General.

"I can assure you, General, you will never see them again."

Henri was the first to protest at being handed over to the Americans.

"Non, mon Général, I prefer to take my chances in front of a French court than to face whatever this American has in mind."

"As would I, mon Général," Paul agreed. "For us the war is over, Paris is free. Please allow us to withdraw into anonymity, I beg you."

Silently, de Gaulle stared out of the window. He watched children running through the streets. Some appeared to be playing war... while others scavenged through the debris left by the Germans for food scraps.

"You guarantee I will never suffer the displeasure of another encounter with this trio, Major Donovan?"

"You can wave them off at the docks in Calais if it makes you happy."

"Then get them out of my office."

"Um, one more thing, General?"

"You are pushing your luck, American," de Gaulle snapped.

"This is something you brought on yourself, Chucky."

The General spun about on his boot, and took a few steps, ready to thrash the impertinent OSS officer for his utter lack of respect. Expecting his subordinate to retreat, de Gaulle came to an abrupt halt when he registered the major, undaunted by the leader of France, had not moved and was wafting a sheaf of papers under his nose.

"Since you had these two arrested this morning... and I am sure the assemblage in the hallway heard you threaten all three with treason... I am going to need you to sign their official pardons for any and all crimes they may have committed for the sake of a Free France. I know President Roosevelt would appreciate it and will make sure to reward your humanitarianism in kind with aid from the US."

De Gaulle snatched the documents, ascribed his signature to all three, and shoved them back into Donovan's hands. "Get them, and yourself, out of my office."

Jack nodded. "As you wish, General."

De Gaulle groused, "And Donovan, if I have my way, I will see you either gone from my city... or dead!"

Wordlessly, the three exited behind Jack and trooped out of the hotel.

While the group stood on the footpath in front of the main doors, Jack checked his watch. "Well, that took an unnecessarily long time."

"Enough of the humour, Jack," Evie's patience was hanging by a thread.

"Oui, American," Paul agreed. "What have you conscripted us into?"

"Right now, I recommend a late lunch." Jack smiled all the same. "We have a long couple of days ahead of us, so I suggest you fill up."

He led them to a waiting olive-drab Chevrolet staff car, where a smartly dressed second lieutenant opened the suicide doors for the group.

Once everyone was squeezed inside, Jack chortled from the front seat, "We know of a good cafe don't we, Evie."

Without a direct order, the lieutenant shifted the car into first and headed to the Café la Fête.

Chapter Eight

The American car drew to a stop at the curb a couple of shops down from the cafe. Alighting, Jack opened the rear door to help out Evie, and both watched the two men who had been sitting with her, scoot across the bench seat to join them on the path.

"I have to get something from the trunk. Madame Rousseau..."

The switch to formality elicited a sarcastic retort from Evie. "So, now you've got what you want, we are no longer on friendly terms?"

Jack chose to ignore that. "...please escort your colleagues inside and find us a table. If you would be so kind as to organise a cup of coffee for me, and feel free to order anything you three might like from the menu. Uncle Sam is picking up the tab."

Evie shook her head at being ordered about. She threw Jack a salute. "Aye, aye, mon capitaine." Pivoting on her heel, she marched off, her back ramrod straight, as Paul and Henri traded confused glances before falling in behind her.

The major watched to make sure they did indeed enter

the cafe. While trusting the trio was essential for this mission to be a success, Jack *had* seen fit to station a couple of his men at the rear of the cafe, on the off chance his guests decided to find another place to eat... without him.

Retrieving his briefcase from its secure hiding place, he followed them in.

The cheerful chime above the door, announcing the entrance of a much needed customer caused every member of staff to turn. Their artificial smiles soured into genuinely discontented frowns, they did not bother to conceal when they recognised the woman.

Genevieve's appearance precipitated a subdued discussion as to which unlucky soul would have to serve the one person, they dreaded more than the German High Command.

Facing the open door, Evie witnessed none of this.

Wondering what had captured the attention of a suspected enemy of the French Provisional Government, the eyes of those at the other side of the cafe veered in the same direction.

The sight of the two men, one of whom closed the door behind him before clapping his hands together to warm them, prompted the staff to murmur amongst themselves that another dining establishment ought to be suggested... *perhaps one in a French POW camp.*

The manager narrowed his eyes, his brain working. Hard currency, whatever the denomination, trumped all political and moral considerations. Righteous indignation did not make a profit.

He cleared his throat and gave a brusque toss of his head at the new arrivals, prompting straws to be broken. The shortest fated to undertake the undesirable duty of serving these miscreants.

Their muted debate dwindled when the bell chimed a second time.

A tall man joined the group and, if he was accompanying *this* woman, it was fair to assume his distinctly American attaché case contained military secrets.

One of the older staff members shot a fearful glance at the manager, mouthing, "She found herself another ignorant fish and will no doubt bring destruction down on us."

The youngest waiter elbowed her, whispering more loudly than he ought, "Non, Collette, that is the American who arrested her last..."

Hearing him, Jack ordered, "Hey, Guy, since you seem to be the only one here who appreciates repeat customers, how about you scrounge us up a table." Casting an eye about the empty dining room, he suggested, "Perhaps that one in the back corner opposite the kitchen?"

Shock spread across the boy's face hearing the American use his name... *but then do not all Americans refer to other males as guy?* The young man speculated inwardly.

In truth, Jack was wise to the boy's name... and his background. He had vetted every member of the cafe staff well in advance of his meeting with Genevieve Rousseau outside the premises.

It pleased him to learn these people were nothing more than hard working Parisians, if maybe too conservative in nature, even for him.

All the same, the Café la Fête provided neutral ground where Jack could work, away from the scrutiny of General de Gaulle, whose office was only two floors below Jack's. He also felt comfortable that anything the four of them might discuss would not fall into the hands of German Intelligence.

Guy glanced at his colleagues in appeal, but they vanished

without a word. He griped under his breath about killing the lot of them when he was finished.

Without greeting the group, he snatched a handful of menus and escorted them to a table.

Before he could ask for their preferences in coffee blends, Jack said, "Forget those dinky cups and just bring us a pot and some real cups."

Paul watched the boy head into the kitchen, then pinned his gaze on Jack. "What about this fabulous luncheon you promised? Henri and I did not have the luxury of a decent meal before de Gaulle's goons broke into our house this morning… and I for one am ravenous."

Jack gave a boyish grin. "I lied… all I needed was to get you here. Welcome to the world of professional spies, my friend. Besides, once you succeed with your mission, and you reach New York, I promise, you can eat until you explode."

Evie scoffed, "I get the uneasy feeling you will feed us to the sharks on the way across the Atlantic before we are able to catch a glimpse of the Statue of Liberty."

The conversation stopped when the waiter returned with the coffee and four cups.

Even in his contempt, Guy maintained a level of professionalism, hoping to earn a decent tip.

Filling the four cups, without wasting a drop, he placed the pot in the centre of the table, and set each cup, brimming with the cheapest grind the kitchen had to offer which could still be labelled coffee, in front of each customer.

Once he had served the American, he took a modest step back to the man's left, awaiting any additional requests. The way the American was throwing his weight around, Guy assumed he was in charge of this coffee klatch and any meal requests would come from him.

Four pairs of eyes swivelled to the waiter. Unnerved with the attention, the young man began to grow anxious.

"W-would you perhaps wish to see our menu? The quiche our chef prepares actually contains fresh eggs rather than powdered."

"No thank you," Jack replied. "They've already eaten. Just make sure the pot doesn't go empty."

Guy nodded, and turning on his heel, muttered, "Cheap Americans."

In disbelief, Henri slapped his palms on the table, rose to his feet, scowled at Paul and Evie, then vented his outrage at Jack.

"Sir, I will be taking my leave. These two might be fine with your games, but I for one am tired of your... what do you Americans like to say?... oh yes... bullshit." Unknowingly echoing Evie's taunt of the previous night.

Henri glanced at Paul, disappointment in his lover's docility evident. "I have already suffered more than my fair share of subjugation at the hands of the Germans, as well as public humiliation by my fellow countrymen. I have no desire to sit here any longer and allow you to dictate my actions."

"Monsieur Petit, you will sit your ass back in that chair and shut up until I tell you to speak."

"What gives you the right to talk to me that way? I shall see you are reported to your—"

"Sit. Down. Now."

Jack's cold glower left those at the table in no doubt that his genial veneer was dwindling rapidly. He meant business.

Slowly, Henri did as instructed.

Jack opened his attaché case and spread its contents across the table.

From there, the conversation focused on only one thing.

Chapter Nine

P assing the cafe's front window, the manager noticed the heavy winter clouds which had painted all of Paris in shades of grey were streaked with a flash of red fire where the rays of the setting sun cleaved the mass, only to darken once more as the blazing orb sank below the horizon.

To the whimsically minded observer, the dramatic transformation reflected the pervading mood of the city... a glimpse of bright hope, snatched before it could be grasped.

To the manager, it represented the need to rid his long empty establishment of its current occupants in hopes of attracting genuine diners. So far the only money he had generated from the quartet was three pots of coffee.

At first, he believed the heated whispers and accompanying fist pounding on the table, all of which would cease the moment any of the staff dared venture within earshot, might have deterred potential customers.

It was the sight of a shadowy figure slipping away from the light bleeding through the glass which made him realise who the true culprits were.

I cannot believe the arrogant American had the balls to station men along the path to entice my afternoon patrons to seek refreshment elsewhere.

In high dudgeon the manager stormed across the wooden floor to the sole occupied table. Each echoing step amplified his anger. "Monsieur, I insist you and your party finish your business and be on your way. I cannot afford to waste any more time with you."

"By all means, sir." Jack smiled and scooped up the papers, tapping them on the top of the table to straighten the sheaf. "If we could get the bill please… my superiors are sticklers when it comes to accounting for every penny."

The manager was ready for the request, and placed the hand scribbled receipt for fifteen francs next to Jack's cup. He had tried to increase the cost enough to recoup any part of what he had lost throughout the day, but doubted the American would accept the ridiculous check without an argument.

Americans are the same even in the good times.

Jack studied the bill for a moment and nodded. "I don't have any francs on me, would you accept dollars?"

Withdrawing a fifty-dollar bill from his wallet, he offered it to the manager.

"Monsieur, I could not possibly take a bill such as that for payment. We do not have enough currency on hand for the difference."

"Then consider it a tip for the use of your facility. Better yet…" Jack dug out a twenty as well. "…I hope this will cover your losses for today."

To those at the table, quietly awed by the American's unexpected generosity, Jack extended his hand to the door.

"I believe our discussion is concluded for the time being."

The December chill prompted Jack to shove his hands into his pockets as he advised Henri and Paul, "Gentlemen, I suggest you head home to await my call."

Henri was about to express his disagreement at being confined to their house, but Paul placed a hand on his shoulder. Squeezing it gently was his way of silencing his partner.

The pair nodded and began their trek home.

"Oh," Jack's tone brought both men to a standstill. "If either of you had any thoughts of leaving the city, know that your pictures have been distributed to every military checkpoint from the Spanish border to Switzerland."

It was another lie, but the looks on their faces as they exchanged a glance, told Jack they had to believe him.

Without another word, they disappeared into the night.

Satisfied two of his newly formed tactical team were not about to abscond, Jack turned his attention to the remaining member.

"Well, Evie…?"

She interrupted sardonically, "Oh, are we back on a first name basis, Major Donovon?"

Jack brushed off the gibe. "I don't know about you, but I could use something to eat. Whatcha say we find an actual restaurant and have dinner?"

"I confess, because of you I am starving but, while I appreciate the invitation, I cannot say I trust you to keep your word and feed me. What if I was to take you to my favourite bistro?"

Glancing back at the Café la Fête's warmly glowing front glass, Jack asked curiously, "Were we not just there?"

"*Non.*" Evie chuckled. "The food here is atrocious, and why I only bother to meet the enemy there. If your driver is still about, I am sure he will have no problem finding it.

When they drew up to the curb in front of the building, Jack shook his head in humorous disbelief. "I could take you anywhere in the city, but you prefer to eat at home?"

"Yes, as I said before, I want to be assured of getting fed this time, and surmise it has been a while since you have had the pleasure yourself. However, if you don't do the gentlemanly thing and help me out of this car, I might rescind my invitation."

Jack did not need to be reminded of his lack of social graces. He bounded around the Chevy to open Evie's door with an exaggerated flourish.

Outstretching his hand, he flashed a smile. "Allow me, Madame?"

The return grin on Evie's lips was equally wry, "I thought you would never ask."

Linking his arm through hers, Jack escorted her up the old and worn stone steps. At the top, he was about to turn the brass knob, when the touch of her slender fingers caused him to pause.

Evie nodded at the dark car parked a little way down the street. "Unless you wish to invite my chaperones to join us, how about giving them the evening off? I am sure they too are famished."

Jack contemplated denying any knowledge of her being under surveillance, but the gleam in her eye told him it would be a waste of breath.

Circling his hand above his head, he signalled to the occupants to wrap it up for the night.

Headlights off, the driver executed a neat U-turn. Evie and Jack saw the flash of red, as the car slowed and took a road to the left, vanishing from view.

Unhooking her arm from Jack's, Evie turned the knob to let them into the dimly lit, sparsely inhabited building.

"Shouldn't a single woman, all alone in Paris be more

cautious about her safety and lock up when leaving? What about your tenants, don't they ever think to secure your front door?" Jack asked, genuinely concerned.

Evie shrugged, and shut the door behind them. "Why bother when we have the world's best security system on our doorstep twenty-four hours a day? The only person I am concerned about breaking into my apartment is you."

One foot on the bottom stair, she added. "I am sure you already have one but, just in case, do not let me forget to give you the spare key."

With no time to mask his shock, Jack was caught off guard by the offer.

Ascending the curving staircase, Evie concluded, "Do not think that is an open invitation for you to visit anytime you want. I just do not have the funds to replace the locks every time your men break in."

Chapter Ten

The aroma of roasting chicken made Jack's stomach rumble as he waited for Evie to finish preparing their meal.

His ear to the kitchen door, he listened carefully to ensure his hostess was where she was supposed to be, especially as this morning, she had effected an escape, which would have made Houdini proud.

Quietly taking a step back, Jack repeated his earlier offer, "Are you sure you do not need any help in there? The army taught me how to peel a mean potato."

From her position on the other side of the door, where she had spent the last ten minutes hearing Jack wander through her parlour, Evie replied, "*Non*, I am almost done. If you have managed to find the liquor cabinet, could you pour me something to drink?"

Jack winced at the accusation but, like a child caught by his mother, red-handed in the cookie jar, he could not deny it. Snooping was an occupational habit. It came as naturally as breathing.

He had already studied the photographs on the shelves.

He did not bother to ask who the black and white images belonged to, being well-versed with her family history, dating back to her great grandparents' participation in Napoleon's march from Golfe-Juan in the south to Paris to reclaim his throne after his initial exile.

From there, he had perused her books. Coming across a tattered and dog-eared first-edition copy of Marx's *Communist Manifesto* left him mildly perturbed. From what Jack knew of Evie's late husband, he guessed it had belonged to him.

This must be required reading, he reasoned, replacing it neatly. *Especially if you aim to be a proper Socialist in France.*

Trying to cover his tracks, Jack scuffled through the room as though fulfilling her request.

"Where do you keep it?" he raised his voice to ask.

"In the cupboard under the books you have no doubt been leafing through."

"Does that woman have x-ray vision?" Jack mumbled to himself.

Opening the cupboard doors, the only alcohol he found was a couple of bottles of red and white wine... neither of which had French labels.

Hearing the clink of glassware, Evie pushed through the door between the two rooms, bearing a tray of chicken and small potatoes.

"I apologise for my lack of suitable spirits, but our prior overlords laid claim to the bulk of our harvest, and your captain thought it would impress me to serve *imported* wine from Californian vineyards."

"The man should be shot without recourse," Jack chuckled. "Red or white?"

"That question alone should earn you a bullet as well. We are having chicken and potatoes... so, white, of course. Do they teach you soldiers nothing about how to mingle with civilised cultures?"

Pouring a glass of wine, Jack stood it alongside her plate, then poured another for himself. "Nope, only how to blow things up and kill other soldiers."

"Well, tonight, there will be no such conversations. Sit and enjoy."

"Before I do, may I put a record on your Victrola? A little dinner music would be nice."

Jack had already searched the Victrola's cabinet, and knew what he wanted to listen to first. Flipping open the wooden lid, he placed the shellac record onto the turntable.

The unit's crank wound, and the needle set in place, the age of the machine became apparent when the Victrola brought the instrumental lead into Teddy Wilson's piano solo crackling to life.

Resuming his seat at the table, he raised a toast to his hostess as Billie Holiday eased into *If You Were Mine*.

With a clink of Evie's mother's cherished wine glasses, the two partook of the late evening meal.

Between bites, Evie decided to revive a mood which seemed to be stagnating. "Funny story behind that old player. One of our former tenants listened to it at all hours of the day or night, which irritated my mother no end."

"Did your mother hate music?"

"No, just the tenant."

"Then why did the tenant hand over something of such value?"

"He fell behind on his rent. So, my father, the good soul he was, agreed to forgive the man's debt in exchange for the Victrola and his entire record collection.

"My mother was livid when a group of men in the building appeared on our doorstep with it in tow. My father, of course, in the lead carrying a stack of records. I can still hear Maman threatening Papa."

Even though there was no way Jack could know what her mother sounded like, Evie mimicked her reaction, just in case Maman happened to be listening from Heaven.

"Auguste, you should begin praying the good Lord has made those things edible, because they will be your dinner from now on."

Jack could not help laughing at the image Evie conjured up.

Happy she had succeeded in her ploy, Evie continued, "Father set the records to one side, and curbed her admonishment by dint of sweeping her into his arms for a kiss. Hopeless romantic. When she was in one of those moods, Papa knew sweet talking would not win her over. As much as she tried to deny it, his embrace and kiss melted her to the point where her only recourse was to throw up her hands in disgust and march off."

"It sounds like you grew up in a loving home," Jack observed as Billie Holiday's band played her out. The record clicked, a signal they needed to change it.

Jack half-rose, but Evie beat him to it. He watched as she crouched to rummage through the stack.

"Would you like to hear their favourite recording?" she asked diffidently.

"Uh, sure," Jack answered, uncertain whether the question was rhetorical.

Slender legs lifted Evie upright, her oversized skirt flowing about them.

The scratchy sound of a well-played 78 filtered through the speaker.

Hearing the familiar melody, a tear trickled down her cheek as the memories of her parents flooded her unexpectedly. Ridding it with the back of her hand, she sighed softly.

"I would peek from my bedroom door and watch the two of them dance.

"Their performance was comical to me but, to each other, they were Fred Astaire and Ginger Rogers."

Adrian Rollini's combo led into Ella Logan's sultry declaration: *It had to be you.*

Feeling the touch of Jack's hand on her shoulder, Evie turned to find herself in his arms.

Maybe it's the wine or the longing to be held by someone... Genevieve could not be certain which... but she had no reservations about melding against Jack in a slow dance.

Why this man? Her subconscious tried to rationalise. *He lacks Paul's empathy, and definitely does not measure up to my Claude. Still...*

As the chorus began, Evie realised her head was resting on Jack's chest. She thought she heard the quickening of his heartbeat.

At the end of the song, the old needle got caught in an unseen scratch, repeating the same line... *With all of your faults, I love you still.*

Her gaze caught Jack's.

Overwhelmed by the moment, Evie closed her eyes as Jack drew her into a kiss. Neither had planned it, providence had bestowed it on the strange couple.

Slowly, Evie broke from the kiss, and Jack's embrace. She walked over to the Victrola, lifting the arm, silencing the melody.

Uncharacteristically irresolute as to the next move, Jack remained rooted to the spot. When she failed to retrace her steps, he looked at his watch.

"Goodness, is that the time," he noted casually. "I thoroughly enjoyed dinner tonight. You are indeed an excellent cook, Madame Rousseau. Please allow me to take my leave, I have an early morning."

Evie forced herself to rein in her emotions. "By all means, Major Donovon. Will we be meeting tomorrow?"

"It depends on the intel I'm expecting to receive. I shall let you know."

Gathering his coat, Jack walked to the door. His hand on the latch, he murmured without turning, "Thank you, again. Have a pleasant night, Evie."

At the quiet thunk of the door closing, Evie's legs gave out. Clutching the edge of the Victrola's wooden cabinet, she collapsed to her knees, her forehead coming to rest against it, as she sobbed uncontrollably.

Chapter Eleven

14th December 1944
Morning

It had been almost five days since their dinner 'date' had ended awkwardly. Neither had reached out to the other for fear of having to confront what had occurred.

Worse, in Jack's case, he had broken a cardinal rule.

Even now, as he scanned the same documents for the hundredth time, his only thought was Evie.

His conscience cursed him again for stepping over the line. *Dammit, man, you can sleep with any woman you want, any time you want. How could you be stupid enough to think it would be okay to do so with her? Hell, you do not even know whether you can trust her.*

His heart's rebuttal was passionate. *You saw her... her frailty... her loneliness. She has lost so much in this goddamn war. Is it so wrong to offer some comfort, to indulge in a night... or ten... of pleasure? To show her not every man in Paris is out to—*

Is out to what? Jack's conscience interrupted. *Use her? You are already doing that, aren't you? Be man enough to admit, you were thinking with your dick, eager to bed her.*

As much as Jack tried to rationalise the situation... it was true. If she had returned to his arms or simply turned around, he would have grovelled at her feet and, had she invited him to, followed her to bed like a puppy on a lead.

Needing to get his head together, he promised himself to call on Evie soon but, for today, he had more pressing war-related details requiring his concentration.

Which meant paying a visit to the one person he found even more repugnant than French General Windbag, who would no doubt be too busy sucking the life out of everyone in his office on the ground floor to accord Jack's needs any attention.

Major Jackson Donovon, United States Third Army, stood motionless outside the door which had, at one time, served as the hotel's Presidential Suite. His cap was tucked under his arm, respectfully, as taught in boot camp, although he was not sure it should matter.

He had chosen to take the stairs down from his office to the suite below, deliberately, giving him extra time to practice being contrite. However, no amount of feigned sincerity could conceal his contempt for the arrogant bastard.

Staring at the decorative double doors separating him from the resident on the other side, Jack failed to comprehend why the man had been allotted such luxury.

The sentries on either side looked at each other nervously, silently trying to determine what the American was doing.

Hesitantly, the young lieutenant asked, "Have you business with the Général, Major?" The man's Senegalese-French accent was rich and distinctive. "I do not recall being informed to expect anyone."

Jack shook his head. "No, he isn't expecting me, but it is imperative I speak with him."

"I am sorry, sir, he is in the middle of a crucial debriefing and left orders not to be disturbed. Perhaps if you were to contact Général de Gaulle's aide-de-camp I am—"

Already knowing he had worn thin his welcome with Colonel Mattheu Garnier, Jack feared pressuring the man any more could be counterproductive for when he really needed help.

"I'm sorry, I know you are only doing your job, but I have neither the time nor the energy to play political tag." Jack reached for the knob, to find his hand removed... forcibly.

"Please forgive me, Major. I am sure the problem can wait unti—"

Jack lost his patience and, being Jack, was not about to let a member of the French colonial troops hinder him. Brushing off the hand, he tried to shove his way through, which resulted in a tussle.

A disturbing realisation hit Jack while the two struggled for dominance. *Even today, there were places in the world where, despite the numbers of black soldiers fighting for their respective countries, this man would be arrested for laying his hands on a white man in the course of defending his post.*

A prejudice he could not fathom.

It shocked him into relinquishing his grip, feeling each rosette, meticulously carved in the panel, biting into his back as the sentry slammed him against the solid oak door. Fortunately for Jack, the soldier's compatriot intervened.

"Aliou, enough. You are as much a nuisance as this fool."

By then, it was too late. The door swung open and Jack stumbled backwards into the arms of somebody behind him.

Looking up, Jack saw the pudgy face of the former

German Governor of Paris, General de Infanterie Dietrich von Choltitz, staring down at him.

Contrary to his usual finely tailored army uniform, the general sported a pair of red silk pyjamas, creating the impression he was a sultan awaiting his latest concubine.

The man's calm and polished demeanour was not one expected of a defeated warrior.

Jack was envious of the fact Choltitz appeared well rested, biding his time until transport could be arranged to spirit him away to London and the cozy confines of Trent Park.

He hated the very thought of that place. The luxurious country estate served as a *detention centre* for those select few self-serving Nazi officers sent to wait out the war in splendour while innumerable lives on both sides continued to be sacrificed.

Jack knew it was unlikely these narcissistic traitors to their sworn cause would see the inside of a courtroom for their atrocities because they coughed up valuable information in exchange for avoiding the hangman's noose.

Christ, Jack grouched inwardly, *we should just rid the world of them the moment they arrive and bury their bodies where no one will ever find them.*

Hoisting the American upright, Choltitz placed his dangling monocle against his right eye, and greeted his unexpected guest with a sardonic smile.

"Ah, if it is not my favourite interrogator, Major Donovon. To what do I owe this surprise visit? Perhaps, you need to get in a last minute torture session before I am shipped out? Perhaps the Senegalese soldiers on the other side of the door would be happy to assist. I hear they prefer to use machetes to do their handiwork."

The irony of having two African soldiers... especially those of the Senegalese Army... preventing Choltitz from leaving his room was not wasted on Jack. The Germans, to whom this particular army represented a source of cultural disdain, had massacred some forty of their countrymen in Chasselay during their push through France in June of 1940.

Their ancestors had defeated the Kaiser's stormtroopers, soundly, in combat, thwarting potential German advances during the Great War. This generation's offence, besides being black, was refusing to surrender until the last of their ammunition was spent. To underline their hatred of these troops, the Germans chose to leave the white English officers who had commanded them, unharmed.

Glaring at his *attendants* with undisguised loathing, the general ushered Jack in, and shut the wooden doors with a solid thud.

Straightening his uniform, Jack waited for an invitation to sit.

The general returned to his typewriter and continued to commit his thoughts to paper, without bothering to offer Jack as much as a *fuck you.*

Ignoring his host's discourtesy, Jack made a bee-line for the liquor cabinet. Grabbing a crystal snifter, he uncorked its matching decanter and poured himself a generous measure of cognac.

"Where are my manners?" He reached for a second glass. "Do you want one?"

His eyes on the keys, Choltitz replied, "I am sure I will need more than that by the time you are finished... but let me start with one."

Filling the snifter, Jack wandered behind the general and began to read as he typed.

"Did not your mother teach you how impolite it is to read over someone's shoulder?"

"Never came up. My mom didn't care much for books." Jack placed the drink next to the typewriter. Without asking permission, he picked up the neatly stacked pile of completed pages from their storage box to Choltitz's right.

Thumbing through them, he chuckled. "Is it not a trifle early to be writing your memoirs?"

"Not at all, major. One must keep one's mind sharp during these extended periods of inactivity."

"Then allow me to ask, did *your* venerable Saxon mother neglect to teach you that telling lies is the quickest path to Hell."

Jack filled his mouth with the aromatic spirit waiting for the German to respond, but the general refused to be bated.

Jack goaded, "See, right here for instance…"

He smacked the page he was reading, and the scrunch of crumpling paper filled the room. "Really? Despite your dedicated service to the Third Reich, you regard yourself as merely a faceless cog in the party's apparatus? And here… you endeavour to justify your actions as those of an innocent civil servant?

"Take this line for example."

Jack cleared his throat, mocking Choltitz with a bad German accent, "Mein only concern as governor of the historically rich city of Paris was to protect its treasures and citizens from the evil of the German High Command in Berlin.

"That would be downright humorous if it weren't so far from the truth. I wonder if the dead of Rotterdam thought you were serving *their* humanitarian need?"

The statement arrested the incessant tap of the typewriter's keys.

The general's sorely tested forbearance had run out. He spun around in his chair. "You have exactly thirty seconds, Major Donovon, to explain why you are bothering me before I summon de Gaulle's pet gorillas in the hallway and have you lobbed head first through one of this magnificent hotel's sadly broken windows."

Dropping the manuscript into the box, Jack perched on the edge of the desk.

"Fine, if you do not wish to hear my constructive criticism of your writing style, tell me where the cache of weapons and explosives your garrison did not have time to claim, is hidden."

Choltitz sighed. "For the love of God, man. As I spent three days telling you, the last time I could not avoid speaking with you, the weapons are gone. Destroyed... as you Americans are so fond of saying... poof in a cloud of smoke."

"Come now, General, we both know that is a lie. The French army could find no trace of your weapons' depot, nor did the partisans claim to have them in their possession."

Returning to his writing, the general said nonchalantly, "Believe me or not, Donovon, I can only tell you what I know. I apologise for your wasted trip down from your cubby hole, but it is time you took your leave."

Jack pushed himself off the desk and, out of habit, straightened his uniform again. Without so much as a salute or a farewell, he marched to the door, his stride, a recognisable military cadence.

Over the nonstop tap of keys being struck on his typewriter, Choltitz spoke, "A word of advice, if I could not obtain weapons from Mon Général Asparagus downstairs, I would ask that weasel working for you... what was his name again... oh yes, Henri Petit."

It was Jack's turn to swing around. "How do you know about Petit?"

"Monsieur Petit managed to skim enough weapons and ammunition from our shipments to propagate and arm both sides of the war, I am sure will be waged between Norway and Sweden once all this is finished.

"I know if I was King Haakon, I would be out for Swedish blood bearing in mind their alleged neutrality." Choltitz scoffed, "Or should I say Swedish nationalistic profiteering."

Chapter Twelve

Paul stared out of the window in disbelief.

For the past three days, no fewer than three US army jeeps had been stationed along the road outside the house Henri and he shared.

Each vehicle sported a fifty caliber machine gun, and was manned by some young American eager to release a hail of metallic fury, should any in the vicinity risk poking their heads out of their doors.

This morning, Paul — a strong Zitterkaffee in hand, the same coffee served exclusively by the Germans in their air raid shelters to mollify its citizens suffering from the jitters induced by the continual Allied bombings, and the brand of which Henri had somehow requisitioned about a hundred cases for their personal use — noticed the street was suspiciously clear.

He took a cautious sip to test whether Henri had seen fit to spice the drink with any sort of hallucinogens in an effort to ease Paul's nerves all the more.

Satisfied his lover had not drugged him, Paul ventured to the door, opening it warily. True to his first glance, the street was devoid of any military vehicles, save the old Morris CS8, Henri had purloined after the British Expeditionary Forces abandoned countless scores of the little trucks when they fled the shores of Dunkirk.

"Henri, Henri," he shouted excitedly at his slumbering housemate. "Get up, get up. Gather what you can; we are packing the truck and fleeing Paris."

Henri dragged himself out of their bedroom, his robe askew as he scratched his belly, sleepily. Through a yawn, he asked, "What are you blathering about?"

"Quickly, get dressed and packed. Our opportunity to escape this nightmare has presented itself."

Henri snatched Paul's cup and swallowed the dregs of the rewarmed liquid, hoping it would clear his foggy brain enough to understand Paul's incessant prattling.

"Are you out of your mind? Even if we manage to elude the firing squad outside, you heard the American, there are no safe border crossings for us."

"You forget he said from Spain to Switzerland. The idiot gave us the perfect route. He wants us to go to Luxembourg, so we will go… just without him… and this instant! Now do as I say and pack."

Unsure whether he believed their freedom was at hand, Henri took one step further and swung open the door. Expecting a sputter of American gunfire for his defiance, Henri instinctively flinched to cover himself, to be met with nothing more sinister than the twitter of a pair of late migrating song thrushes perched in a tree along the street.

Straightening himself, Henri grasped the significance of Paul's excited commands. Not bothering to shut the door, he began scooping up any contraband he could lay his hands on, and shuffled to the truck.

While Henri loaded items he thought would aid in their flight — either to trade with or survive on — Paul concentrated on the more durable items such as clothing, papers… and weapons.

As he made his way to the truck, Paul caught sight of his lover's robe still flapping in the morning breeze.

"Dammit, Henri, would you please get dressed? I will finish packing."

The chastisement was unnecessary. The adrenaline which had gripped Henri in the earlier excitement had ebbed, replaced by the knowledge that his manhood was being accosted by the December winds.

Tugging his robe shut, he hurried into the house to do as Paul bade.

Paul stashed a Walther P.38 along with the official papers Henri had procured when the Germans fled the city. He never questioned how his man obtained the things he had.

In war, it is better never to ask certain questions.

The minutes Paul suffered through awaiting Henri's return, felt more like hours until, frustrated by the tardiness of his housemate, he stomped inside.

"Henri, you had better *not* be taking a bath!"

Fighting the impulse to haul Henri out of the house by his ear, Paul elected to drag him down the path to the truck by his arm, while Henri struggled to button his shirt.

"For the love of the Blessed Virgin, Paul, I am moving as fast as I can," Henri objected. "The street is still clear. The American must have lost interest in us. I'll wager he is too busy canoodling with Genevieve. In any case, we have plenty of time for me to get dressed. So, kindly, let go of me." He shrugged off Paul's hand.

"Fine," Paul sighed. "As long as you quit dallying and get in the truck."

"Boys, boys," from the back of the vehicle, a Midwest-American drawl greeted the pair, bringing both to a standstill.

Peeking around the side, Paul and Henri discovered Jack sitting on the edge of the truck bed.

"It appears you put your time to good use and gathered the supplies required to track down the Germans.

"Daniel here..." Jack nodded at the canvas-covered depth of the vehicle, from where a slender man, sporting a German StG44 machine gun, appeared.

"...oh, excuse me, please allow me to introduce Staff Sergeant Daniel Fisher of the US 2nd Battalion, 30th Infantry. Anyway, he was betting the two of you were trying to do something stupid like running away. I told him he was wrong. In fact, I went so far as to reprimand Daniel with severity for *daring* to utter such disparaging criticism."

Glancing at his companion, Jack smiled. "Remember to apologise to these fine patriots."

Daniel grunted and jumped down from the truck, heading for the passenger side of the vehicle. Glaring at Paul and Henri, he climbed inside and banged the door shut.

"I guess losing ten francs on you two has left him a trifle surly. You can discuss it with him when you collect the rest of these items."

Jack held out a tattered sheet of paper on which was scribbled a list of various odds and ends.

Henri accepted it and scanned it quickly. His mouth dropped open when he reached the bottom.

"How do you propose I rustle up American M1's and rifle grenades? Do you expect me to wander into a market or maybe mail order them?"

"Not my problem, Henri, but I do expect you to be at Madame Rousseau's building by midnight tonight ready to roll out."

In fluent French, a command was snapped at the trio, "Pouvons-nous déjà commencer?" (Can we get going already?)

Henri and Paul stood agape when they realised it came from the American in the front seat.

Jack chuckled, "Did I forget to mention Sergeant Fisher's family migrated to the US from the Bordeaux region? Not only can he speak French, but also he's adept at recognising a good bottle of wine.

"Enough of the references." He put an end to the niceties. Pulling his .45 from its holster, he aimed it at the duo, then pointed the barrel at the lowered tailgate.

"If you will, Monsieur Petit, I would like you to climb into the back of the truck and act as navigator while Paul drives.

"And if either of you come up with the crazy notion to make a break for it, be aware that Daniel is a pretty good shot as well."

Chapter Thirteen

As the Morris truck bounded along the potted dirt road to some obscure location outside Paris, Staff Sergeant Fisher cursed ever running into Major Jack Donovon.

While he kept an ear tuned into the conversation between his two wards, Daniel thought back to that fateful day.

His squad was part of Patton's Third Army's push east towards Paris. Assigned to act as reconnaissance, they had advanced deep into enemy held territory.

Outside the small town of Dreux, he and his men had come across an American arguing with a French farmer, on the road leading to the town's square. The man was out of uniform and definitely ought not to have been there.

Daniel had stopped his troop, to eavesdrop on the conversation.

Although the American spoke French it was barely passable, and it was obvious the farmer could not understand his badly phrased questions.

"Paris, man, how far is it?" exhorted the American.

"I have told you before this is not Paris," the farmer retorted.

"I am well aware of that. I want to know where...?"

"For the last time, you are in Dreux not Paris. Are you suffering from shell shock or something? Do you want me to take you to a doctor for your head?"

Stepping forward, Daniel had interceded for the lost American. His rifle held to the ready just in case the stranger was not from the same side of the battle as he and his men.

"Please excuse my confused countryman, sir." His accent had made the farmer smile. "I believe he has either lost his way to the City of Lights, or he wants to sleep with your prized hog. Who can really tell?"

The two men had shared a laugh at Jack's expense. Good-humouredly, the farmer had replied, "Tell your friend he would be best served following this road to a Paris book-store. If need be, I would be happy to donate a few francs to buy him a decent French primer."

"As tempting as that offer is, monsieur, your generosity in providing directions to the poor sap is more than he could hope for."

The two men shook hands, then Fisher had nudged Jack with the barrel of his rifle, and in a thick Brooklyn accent, said, "After you."

As the group trudged along, Daniel had observed, "I guess by your terrible French, your German is just as bad. Army Intelligence?"

With a wry smile, Jack had introduced himself. "Major Jack Donovon."

"Well, Dorothy, you're not in Kansas anymore," Daniel had wisecracked. "I suggest you stick with us until the rest of the Third Army catches up."

"I can see you are a useful chap to know."

Daniel had no idea his invitation would ensnare him in Jack Donovon's web, contending one of his ancestors had been served a better deal during the French Revolution for supporting King Louis XVI.

He only lost his head to the guillotine.

The ill-fated meeting had cost Daniel the one thing more valuable to him than his neck, something he had worked tirelessly towards since enlisting in the service before the war… becoming a platoon leader.

Without any say in the decision, Staff Sergeant Daniel Fisher found himself transferred to a desk in some clandestine OSS office serving as a translator.

An unexpected hole in the dirt road jostled Daniel out of his reverie; the barrel of his machine gun jamming painfully into Paul's ribs.

"Watch where you are shoving that thing, man," Paul snapped.

"Stow it. You didn't get shot," Daniel retaliated.

At the sound of the front seat occupants bickering, Henri poked his head through the canvas flap separating them.

"If you did not have your damned gun, I would snap your neck like a twig, American," Paul snarled.

"Bring it on, Frenchie. I'd rip you in two… barehanded."

Ever the diplomat, Henri realised he needed to intervene. With a light chuckle, he chastised Daniel for his poorly chosen barb. "Frenchie, eh? It appears Americans have been a bad influence on you. From where in France does your family hail?"

Paul glared at Henri's peaceable intervention, and flipped his hand angrily.

Still wanting to feed the driver the butt of his rifle, Daniel humphed, "Somewhere in southern France. They produced wine."

"Is that so? What was the winery called?"

"I doubt you would recognise the name… Fuschia Win—"

"Fuschia Wines? I heard that vineyard produced some of the best wines in the south of France. I have searched for years in hopes of finding a surviving bottle. Why ever did your family decide to give up tending vines?"

"The choice was made for them by the Great French Wine Blight. Perhaps you know about it? The remedy for the damn aphids came too late for my family to save our lands."

"Truly a pity, Sergeant Fisher," Henri commiserated.

"We have always dealt with antisemitism," Daniel reflected. "Who'd have thought such a tiny bug could be more insidious."

The pair looked up as the truck slewed to a halt.

Engaging the hand brake, Paul said, "If you are done getting to know each other and, unless your directions were wrong, Henri, we are here."

The trio studied the ramshackle farm spread out before them. A lone man stood on the drive. His thick, dark moustache and deeply tanned skin attested to his Romani heritage.

Had they but known it, the Romani was only a child when his group were hounded from the Austro-Hungarian Empire at the end of the nineteenth century for daring to hunt on the Emperor's lands.

Since arriving in France, he and his people had eked out

an existence selling and trading items they had *acquired* by any means necessary. The French and the Germans had found their services convenient, turning a blind eye to their existence.

Their uncompromising reputation was merited.

"Why, Henri? Why are we dealing with these people?" Paul quizzed, his expression one of distaste.

"Paul, you know as well as I, if there is anything available on the black market, the gypsies have it in their possession." Henri patted Paul's forearm in reassurance, hopped down from the back of the Morris and paused at the driver's door.

Without taking his eyes off the gypsy, he instructed Paul, "Stay put and keep the engine running. This should not take long."

Approaching the man as though they were old friends, Henri gave the Romani a comradely hug and kissed his cheeks.

The gypsy tolerated the cordial French greeting because there was money on the table and, overlooking the unwelcome familiarity, questioned Henri's presence at his farm.

Paul and Daniel watched the gypsy nod and point at the dilapidated barn. They saw Henri look past the man in the same direction and acknowledge whatever he had been told.

Henri gesticulated wildly, which the pair in the truck supposed was all part of how the price was negotiated.

No matter the number of fingers Henri lifted, the swarthy Romani shook his head, responding in kind, apparently demanding more. At last, with a look of disgusted impatience at the, presumably, paltry offers, the gypsy turned his back on Henri.

In what looked to the observers as a bid to prevent the man from leaving, Henri cupped a hand around his upper arm.

Without warning, the Romani swivelled around, pulling a knife from the sheath on his belt. Before Henri could defend himself, the man plunged the blade into his chest.

In shock, Henri looked down at the wound and, in slow motion, crumpled to his knees, before collapsing onto the dirt.

Aggressively, the gypsy thrust his knife at the men in the vehicle, as though in tacit warning that if they decided to exact revenge, the consequences would be the same.

Daniel was the first out, his machine gun at the ready to kill the Romani. A burst of gunshots from the barn's hayloft had him diving under the truck for cover.

In a blind rage, Paul popped open the glovebox and retrieved his pistol. Alighting, he used the door as a shield. Balancing the gun on the edge of the open window frame, he took aim at the retreating attacker.

The gypsy was fleeing at full speed to the barn door. Just as he reached for the handle a *crack* rang out. Paul's bullet sank into the man's back, throwing him against the faded wood. Lifeless, he slithered to the ground.

More gunfire rained down on them, earning an exchange from both Daniel and Paul until, abruptly, the barrage ceased. The silence was just as deafening.

Heedless of his own safety, Paul ran to Henri's inert body, seeing the blood pooling on the ground. Gently turning him onto his back, Paul tore open his lover's shirt and made a valiant attempt to stem the flow.

Henri's eyes fluttered open and, with the last of his strength, reached up to caress Paul's cheek.

95

"A w-wasted endeavour, my love," Henri husked.

"Do not dare die on me, Henri Petit. You promised to grow old with me."

A sweet smile, tinged red at its corners from the blood trickling over his lips, curved Henri's mouth.

"Dearest, this war has made old men of us all," he rasped.

The last breath of Henri Petit carried his eternal pledge, "But know I will wait for you—"

Tears spilled down Paul's cheeks as he closed Henri's vacant stare with loving fingers. Hearing the crunch of footsteps, he spun about, his pistol ready to take the life of whoever it might be.

Daniel stopped in his tracks, his hands thrown up. "Whoa, whoa, it's me."

"You… you and your friend caused this," Paul accused, and cocked the pistol's hammer. "Give me one good excuse not to shoot you."

"Look, I'm sorry he got himself killed—"

"How was this Henri's fault, you bastard? He would have never been here, if not for Donovon!"

"Exactly, Paul, because of Donovon. I am as much his prisoner as you, but I know the man well, and his judgement is sound. I'm pretty sure if we don't complete this mission, France will be brought to her knees by something so heinous, she will never be able to recover.

"So the choice is yours, soldier. Either leave Henri where he is and help me make sure his death wasn't for naught or pull the trigger and put *me* out of my hell. In either case, I'm done talking to you."

Without waiting for Paul to respond, Daniel raised his weapon and advanced towards the barn, senses on high alert in anticipation of a renewed rattle of gunfire.

Paul wailed, "Please American do not make me leave him here. He deserves a decent burial."

Keeping his eyes on the barn, Daniel yelled, "Put him in the back of the truck and then get your ass over here.

Daniel advanced on the gypsy, prone in the frigid dirt. The blood staining the back of his jacket, between his shoulder blades, attested to Paul's neatly placed shot. He prodded the body with his boot just to be sure he was dead.

A drop of blood splattered Daniel's cheek. He looked up to see a body sag, then slump over the frame of the hay door. The extent of the head wound confirmed this was his kill.

Swearing under his breath, Daniel swiped off the blood with the sleeve of his coat, then cautiously swung open the barn door.

Expecting all hell to break loose, he was greeted by a deathly silence. Creeping inside, he froze, stunned at the sight which met his gaze.

The interior resembled a military supply depot.

Lined up against the far wall, trucks, jeeps, and staff cars sporting German, Italian, French, and American insignias. Each looked as though they were fresh off a transport train.

In one of the stalls, Daniel spied crates stamped with a German eagle clutching a swastika. Unable to read German, he could tell the boxes contained weapons, and the crates to their right stacked with ammunition.

Grabbing a crowbar from a hook, he wrenched open a couple until he found the cartridges for his particular rifle.

In the next stall, he discovered five crates labeled *M1 Garand Rifles* earmarked for 442nd Infantry Regiment.

"Guess the gypsies figured we wouldn't miss a few cases. Fucking thieves," Daniel griped.

As he continued to search for the rifles, ammo, and anti-tank grenades, Daniel heard Paul enter the barn.

Waving him over to the stall, he thought he should apologise for his earlier remark. "Hey, I'm sorry for sounding so callous. I can't imagine what you're going through—"

Paul raised his palm. "What is the saying? In war, good men die. I will see his death is avenged. Until then, let us find what we were sent here for and return to Paris. I want to leave before the rest of the scum decide to come looking for their comrades."

Chapter Fourteen

Late Evening

Trepidation filled Jack while he ascended the stairs to Evie's apartment, his hand jingling the set of keys in his pocket. With each step, he willed the one key he knew was not on his keyring to — by some miracle — manifest... the promised key to her front door.

Even though the proposition was barely more than an off-hand comment made when they were not on such an awkward footing, tonight, Jack surmised it was the only way he would be granted entry.

The building grew quieter the higher he climbed. The handful of remaining tenants inhabited the apartments on the lower levels.

Reaching the topmost landing, he scanned the hallway and, despite knowing these residents had long since been removed by the Gestapo, was convinced he could hear remnants of ghostly conversations echoing along the empty corridor.

Before he plucked up the courage to knock, Jack uttered a

silent plea, "Lord, please let some kind soul be waiting behind these walls, prepared to intervene for me."

His entreaty met dead air.

Then... a wisp of a breeze tickled Jack's ear. Had God decided at this precise moment to break his long quietude?

He swore it countered, "No, Jack, this is your burden to shoulder and resolve."

Dismissing the notion, Jack rapped on the scuffed wood, tentatively. Clasping his hands behind his back, he stood at parade rest and waited for a reply.

None was forthcoming.

His anxiety about facing Evie was transcending into outright fear that she had left him high and dry... and he knew he only had himself to blame.

Jack knocked on the door again. This time, without his previous timidity. In fact, the force was hard enough to rattle the wood in its frame.

Pressing his ear against the panelling, he listened for any sound or movement. The room on the other side remained silent.

"Dammit, Jack," the wisp mocked. "Even I could have told you leaving her to stew in her confusion would give her cause to fle—"

The haranguing vanished into the ether, replaced by the stumbling sounds of Jack's dress shoes scraping across the bare floor when he lurched forwards at the sudden opening of the door.

Whether it was God or Fate who intervened to save Jack from the utter humiliation of sprawling spread-eagled across the threshold, it came at the cost of smacking into Evie.

Catching his footing before he and the slender woman tumbled to the carpet, Jack stammered an apology for his clumsiness.

Evie was not in the mood for his shenanigans.

"For the love of all that's holy, you great gorilla," she took up the lambasting. "I am not sure which irks me more, you trying to break through my door or your physical assault of me in the process."

Military instinct taking over, Jack scrambled to rise to attention and remove his hat in respect. Too late, he discovered it was missing. Worse, it was in the possession of Evie, who used it to hit him in the gut.

As he tried to conceal a wince, Jack recollected the incident at Choltitz's office. *Why the hell does this keep happening to me?*

"Do not stand there gawking," Evie commanded, "just tell me what brings you here tonight, so I can bid you adieu as quickly as possible."

Jack wanted to reach out to her, but it appeared she wanted nothing of the sort.

He offered a contrite, "I came to see how you were..."

"You mean check to ensure I had not left Paris? You have a nerve questioning my word, Jack Donovon? I promised to assist in your endeavour, whatever that entails, so assist you I shall. Then, I can leave this ungrateful city... and you... with a clear conscience."

Jack's heart sank at her declaration. He had never quite been sure what he had expected from her, but the conviction in Evie's words left him reeling.

She crossed the room to her dining room table. "Since you are here, let me show you what *I* have uncovered about the whereabouts of your mystery tanks."

Like an errant schoolboy, Jack took his place next to her, amazed to realise he was looking at a series of American battle maps spread out over the table. Some to which even he had not been privy.

He thought about asking how she had acquired them, but her stern expression curbed his tongue.

Instead, he indicated the section of the French map containing the Ardennes Forest. "According to Military Intelligence, the Germans are massing here... but we already talked about this at the cafe."

"I know we did, Major Donovon, but unlike you these past few days, I have been doing my due diligence. I learned not only something concerning our prey, but also about you."

Evie leant her hip against the table. "Perhaps it is time you told me the truth. Explain why you have pressed my group into service as opposed to being assigned your own squad to hunt down these beasts."

To the rest of the world, Jack had been thoroughly trained to bend the truth to fit his needs. In front of Evie, he slipped up.

Barely a flicker of his eyes, it was something the average person would not have discerned, but Evie had honed her craft in the field and not in a classroom.

Missing the slightest gesture often meant the difference between life and death and, just now, Jack's inability to hold her gaze told her he had more to say.

"Please tell me, Jack, why did your command think you insane for tracking down these ghost tanks? Could it be, they did not believe you?"

"It was more like they felt these tanks represented nothing more than the same feint we pulled on the Germans making them think we were planning to land in Calais rather than Normandy," he muttered, "but, I assure you Patton—"

"Kicked you out of his office and threatened to have you committed to an asylum as a lunatic if you continued to argue your case."

Jack fell silent.

"I *will* tell you the only reason I have not turned you over to your military, besides the fact, you have somehow brainwashed de Gaulle into endorsing your operation, is because you are correct. A few days ago, one of my contacts spotted a column of German tanks stationed in a farmer's field outside Pétange, Luxembourg."

She pointed to a small town on the map, close to the French border.

Jack was elated to know he was right all along, but had to ask, "If they were parked in plain sight, why didn't our reconnaissance spot them?"

"Probably because they were not looking for them. Even if they were, I am guessing the Germans covered them in camouflage so they would not be observed until they needed to be."

Evie retrieved a compass from the table and tapped it against her palm. "I know tanks go boom, but what do you know of their specifications?"

"Over open terrain, they have a range of about 120 miles, on road about 200."

Evie drew a circle representing the maximum range of the Panzers from Pétange.

"What are you playing at, woman?" Jack was puzzled.

Bending to study the map closely, Evie drummed the pencil on the paper, trying to figure out the logic behind launching a military attack from this point.

Marking the towns and villages near the border with small x's, she elaborated, "The Allies occupy too much of this region, and there is nothing left, strategically important enough, to jeopardise these tanks in a frontal assault. I have to agree with your General Patton, Jack. It is simply a ruse."

Without thinking, he snatched Evie's pencil, and stretched over her back. On the boundary of the radius sat a target, she had ignored owing to its distance.

Her eyes widened when he circled it.

Before she could inform him, he was insane for entertaining the possibility, a slurred voice bellowed from the street below.

"American. Show yourself so you can see what you caused."

Jack and Evie hurried to the window. Throwing open the sash, they gaped at Paul who was standing in the Paris night with something large and dark draped over his left shoulder.

Paul took a gulp from the bottle clenched in his right fist. Seeing the two staring at him from above, he shook it at them, erratically, spilling a decent amount of the liquid on himself.

"There you are, you Goddamned murderer," Paul shouted. "Are you satisfied now? Look what you've done to Henri."

His words became incoherent as he wailed, "Henri... Henri... why did you leave me?"

Paul ranted and raved, spouting threats at Jack... of slitting his throat while he slept... or gutting him like trout.

All the while, Daniel was trying to talk sense into the Frenchman. "I *told* you to leave Henri's body in the back of the truck, not parade him through the streets of Paris."

"What do you know, Sergeant?" Paul belched into Daniel's face, eliciting a hand wave from the American to disperse the reek of cheap wine.

Jack instructed, "Get him out of the street! We do not need MP's showing up."

"Exactly where do you suggest I escort him, Major?" Daniel replied sarcastically.

"Put Henri in the Morris and cart Paul's drunk ass up here. What possessed you to buy him a bottle in the first place?"

"I didn't, *sir*," Daniel spat as he struggled to liberate Henri's body from Paul's clutches. "Just like everybody in this damn city. No disrespect, Ma'am..." Daniel nodded at Evie. "...he magically produced one from the depths of the truck."

"None taken, Sergeant Fischer," Evie rejoined. "I imagine, if you looked, you would find more than a few empty bottles back there."

She wanted to giggle at the sight of the two tussling over the body of Henri Petit. She had never particularly liked the man but, out of respect for Paul, she bit her lip.

Finally, in a fit of agitation, Daniel shoved Paul in the chest, and wrested Henri free.

After tucking the body under a tarp in the bed of the truck, Daniel hoisted Paul over his shoulder.

In the middle of spouting obscenities at the Gypsies, Americans, Germans, and the fucking French winter, Paul gave up the ghost and passed out.

"Thank God for small mercies," the sergeant groused, only to add a few expletives of his own as he trudged up the stairs.

Paul spent the remainder of the night in Evie's clawfoot bath, dumped there by Daniel to sleep off his personal alcohol-fuelled wake for his beloved Henri... in case he was visited by the urge to regurgitate the two bottles of wine he had imbibed.

While playing Paul's nanny, Daniel decided to take advantage of Jack and Evie's seemingly endless argument over Jack's sanity. Without them noticing, he locked himself in Evie's bedroom, commandeering an actual featherbed to sleep on for the first time since landing in France.

Chapter Fifteen

15th December 1944
8:24 AM

Morning broke on a cold and dreary dawn. The drizzle, which had fallen off and on throughout the night, returned in a light, steady shower.

Undeterred by the weather, a trio stared into the back of the Morris. The remains within made for a macabre topic of conversation.

Daniel posed the one question no one else wanted to ask, "What are we going to do with his body?"

Jack shrugged. "Well, we can't just drop him off at one of the hospitals in the city, and I do not have the time to file the paperwork for the military to take responsibility." Then murmured for Evie's ears only, "Could we leave him here until—?"

"The hell you will, Jack Donovon," Evie cut him off. "I will not have him getting all puffy and oozy in my apartment."

"But we will see to it—"

Throwing up her hands, she interrupted in an implacable tone, "No means no."

"Then I guess he's coming with us, Sergeant," Jack relented. "Best make room back there for you and Paul so we can hit the road."

"No can do, Major Delusion. Mama Fisher didn't raise her boy to ride in the back of a cold truck... let alone with a corpse. I mean look at him, he's turned blue. If that's not a clear case of rigour mortis, then he froze solid from the cold last night. Either way, I'll be riding up front if you don't mind."

"Come now, Sergeant," Evie tried to reassure Daniel. "It was chilly last night, but I am sure it was not cold enough to freeze Henri."

"Fine, Madame Rousseau, you are more than welcome to accompany him back here then."

"*Sergeant Fisher,*" Jack's tone was of a superior officer about to pull the *Chain of Command* card. "I do not believe I was offering you a choice of seats. Now, get up there and make yourself comfortable." Given he had all but kidnapped Daniel to assist in this venture, Jack was prepared to overlook his subordinate's disrespectful term of address, but the gleam in his eye carried a warning.

That, and the sound of heavy metallic objects clanging together, stifled Daniel's scathing retort.

As one, they turned to see Paul coming towards them bearing a pick and a shovel. He elbowed his way through the huddle to place each piece in the bed of the truck, making sure not to bump Henri.

Curiosity compelled Evie to ask, "From where, in God's name, did you procure those?" She had no idea her father had owned any gardening equipment, he had never lifted a finger to dig anything. "And what do you have in mind?"

Paul scoffed, "Obviously, they were not in your kitchen

cutlery drawer now, were they? I surmised, if they were anywhere in a proper French family's house, they would be in the cellar. And behold, that's where I found them. As for the purpose... I intend to do the very thing the three of you seem either too disrespectful, or cowardly, to undertake."

Climbing into the truck, Paul extended his hand to Daniel, and helped the American up, before turning his attention to Henri's cases, digging through them, until he found a couple of wool blankets to keep the pair warm.

"I'll try not to make it too cozy back here. I am not sure Henri would appreciate it," Paul deadpanned.

Jack and Evie glanced at one another before moving quietly to the cab of the truck. Evie had already claimed the driver's seat as hers, ending Jack's objections with a simple, "Your French is horrendous and I know the roads better than you."

That discussion concluded, she fired up the Morris.

Ignoring Jack's disgruntled eye-roll, Evie ground the gearshift into first and, with a neck snapping jolt, started down the street.

Once she had grasped the *sensitive* nuances of the truck's transmission, Evie manoeuvred the vehicle skilfully along the maze of wet streets through the Parisian neighbourhoods which led to the city's outskirts.

Even in the chill of the early morning, a bead of sweat broke out on her forehead and she held her breath whenever they happened by an American jeep, or when one of the patrols gave the woman driving a British truck, a second glance.

To her relief, none seemed bothered about them. Evidently, according to Jack, it would have been too much of a hassle at this time of the morning, given the night curfew had been lifted.

At the last checkpoint, on the perimeter of Paris, the

Morris was halted by two American soldiers, neither of whom appeared thrilled to be standing in the rain.

The corporal took up position in front of the truck, rifle at the ready, while his lieutenant walked to Evie's door.

Scrutinising the vehicle, the lieutenant barked, "Papers."

She understood the order but looked at Jack all the same.

"Dammit, woman, papers," the man repeated.

Jack smiled and presented *his* papers.

Grateful he did not have to dig out his French translation book, the lieutenant crossed to Jack's side of the truck and took the proffered documents.

In a sincere tone, Jack apologised to the soldier and exacted an ounce of revenge for Evie ridiculing his French.

"I beg your pardon for my driver's inability to understand English. You know how these French are."

"Yeah, I was afraid I might have to resort to drawing pictures in the dirt for her." The soldier shot Evie a snide look.

She did her best to not tell him to go to hell... and take her passenger with him.

"So, Major Donovon, what brings you to our corner of Purgatory?" The lieutenant asked as he returned Jack's papers.

"If I can trust your discretion, Lieutenant, I requisitioned this pretty chippy and her family's truck for a morning's *expedition*."

The lieutenant had learned long ago not to question his superiors.

They are all lazy crackpots, chasing tail instead of fighting, he mused inwardly.

"Aye, sir." He stepped back and saluted, before waving his corporal to stand down.

Before they departed, Jack enquired, "You don't have a field phone connected to HQ with you, by chance."

Guardedly, the lieutenant answered, "Y-yes. Why do you ask?"

Without missing a beat, Jack explained, "Never know when I might come across something out there that ought to be reported."

"Bu-but, Major, I can't just give you mine. It's signed out to me. What happens if *I* need it?"

"I'll have it back before it's missed. Worst case, you can have your NCO over here run and find a phone."

Begrudgingly, the lieutenant relinquished the phone, suspecting the officer would find a way to make his life more of a misery if he argued.

Clear of the checkpoint, the truck rumbled down the road to the border between France and Luxembourg.

Evie shot daggers in Jack's direction.

She was not sure which upset her more, the crack about her lack of English or being labeled a mobile prostitute. Regardless, each earned him a punch in his arm.

She heard him grunt, "What's that for?" …and turned her attention to the road with a satisfied huff, although Jack's previous warning *did* require clarification. "Why didn't he recognise me? I thought you said every checkpoint between Spain and Switzerland was on the lookout for us?"

"Did I?" Jack replied innocently. "I might have exaggerated."

"You mean you lied."

Jack chuckled unrepentantly. "Semantics."

The road between Paris and Reims was clogged with heavy transport vehicles presumably heading to the Ardennes, leaving Evie no alternative but to swerve around them, if she wanted to make any progress.

The congestion remained constant until they reached the western edge of Reims, where the convoy turned north.

Jack frowned. "Looks like the Germans are getting ready to cross the border sooner than I thought."

The traffic on the opposite side of the city was surprisingly quiet. The welcome tranquility went unnoticed by the pair in the front who had begun an earnest debate about how to access the farm, unseen.

A few kilometres outside Reims, an unexpected pounding from the back of the truck curtailed Evie and Jack's deliberations. Slamming on the worn brakes, Evie brought the Morris to a screeching standstill. Flipping aside the canvas, she saw Paul climbing over the back gate, pick in hand.

Hearing the rustle of the heavy material, Daniel swivelled to face Evie long enough to mouth, "I have no idea." Then grabbed the shovel and followed.

Alighting, Evie and Jack watched Paul striding in the direction of a vineyard set back from the road, which appeared to have lain unattended for some time. In the chill of the French winter, the land looked even more desolate, the dormant and gnarled vines creaking in the wind.

To Paul, it was the perfect place.

Deep within the vineyard, he began swinging his pick into the frosty earth. Fortunately, the slightly less frigid temperatures along with the recurring rain of the past few days had left the soil more friable.

Daniel joined him, helping him to dig.

Paul waved him off, resolved to do this himself, but the more he tried to move the American, the more his companion refused to budge. Eventually, Paul relented, and the two men continued in silence. Occasionally, Jack relieved one or the other, while Evie provided water to keep them going.

The group dug for well over an hour before they reached a depth with which they were satisfied.

Daniel and Paul returned to the truck, whereupon Daniel unlatched the tailgate and gave Paul a leg up. He stood quietly, facing away from the dim interior of the Morris... in respect for the final goodbye between the two men.

Daniel felt a tap on his shoulder. Turning around, he helped Paul remove Henri's body.

The pair conveyed him to where Jack and Evie waited.

Wrapped in the tarp from the previous night, Henri was lowered carefully into his final resting place.

It took less time to fill the grave than to dig it. Those who did not have a shovel simply used their hands.

Paul was left with the honour of the last shovelful.

Leaning against the wooden handle of the spade, Paul looked at the mound and eulogised softly, "Wine was your life, my love. I pray God allows you to produce the sweetest grapes in all of France."

Daniel gave Paul a brotherly pat on the back, picked up the tools and, along with Evie and Jack, backtracked to the Morris.

Paul remained for a few minutes, collecting himself. He was still furious with Jack Donovon for sending Henri on so dangerous an errand. That Jack had assisted in the burial process without being asked, mollified him somewhat.

"Farewell, Henri Petit," Paul whispered. He placed a hand on the mound one last time, then followed the others.

Clambering aboard, no one spoke as the truck sputtered to life, resuming its trek to the border.

Chapter Sixteen

By midday, the quartet had arrived at the Luxembourg border.

To the uneducated eye, the crossing looked to have been strengthened and expanded to accomodate the larger vehicles trundling around the countryside. To Jack, it was a deliberate ploy to prevent any line jumping, and ensured no one could avoid the border guards.

The road, on over-engineered concrete supports, spanned a deep drainage culvert which ran at ninety degrees to the crossing and continued in a dead straight line as far as the eye could see in both directions. The two lanes of the bridge were separated by a gap broad enough that all save the widest tyres would become lodged.

Evie braked, and drummed her fingers on the steering wheel, waiting... almost patiently... for someone from the French guard station to challenge their reasons for entering enemy territory.

There was not a soul to be seen.

It appeared to be the same story on the far side of the crossing. No sign of any border guards, German or otherwise. Even more unnerving, not only was the boom gate unmanned, but also it was detached from its post.

"Still think I'm insane?" Jack scoffed. "Wait here." He exited the truck and began, with extreme caution, to walk forwards, searching for signs of booby traps.

Evie's heart leapt into her throat when she saw him come to a sudden stop just beyond the barrier at the French side. She sprang out to chase after him.

"Stay where you are," he snapped. The urgency in his tone brooked no argument, and Evie obeyed without hesitation.

Cautiously dropping to his knees, Jack blew gently on the loose gravel covering the road, exposing a German landmine waiting for some unsuspecting motorist to sneak into the tiny Grand Duchy.

Fishing his Bowie knife from its sheath, Jack eased it around the mine's casing, taking great pains not to disturb the detonator. Freeing the device from its resting place, he carried it to the edge of the road.

With all the strength he could muster, he hurled the deadly bomb, hitting the ground as soon as it left his fingers. Evie did the same.

Landing on its side in the ditch, the landmine unleashed a volley of projectiles. Most were absorbed by the earthen embankment but, despite Jack's pitch being worthy of an outfielder, the blast was powerful enough to fling shrapnel in every direction.

Hot metal fragments peppered the Morris, blowing out the rear tyre and slashing the canvas cover. Daniel and Paul ducked in horror when shards burst through the cloth jettisoning out of the opposite side, narrowly missing them.

As the percussion of the mine echoed off in the distance, Jack rose, dusted himself off, and continued his survey.

Evie sat at the edge of the road, her gaze fixed on the American as he played mine detector, relieved when the other two materialised beside her, demanding to know why they were under attack. She pointed at Jack… the only explanation necessary.

"So much for the element of surprise, eh?" Daniel grunted.

As Jack neared the Luxembourg side, the trio saw him go onto his knees again. At first they considered swarming under the truck for cover. The sight of the punctured tyre changed their collective thinking, and they raced around the back of the guard shack for sturdier shelter.

Peeking around the structure, they watched Jack successfully removed another mine, from the same side of the road as the last.

The shock from the second detonation, though not as pronounced as the first, still startled the three, interrupting their conversation. Providence saw fit to smile down upon them this time.

Due the incline of the land, the ditch at the Luxembourg edge of the crossing was significantly deeper than its French counterpart, and all the shrapnel was contained therein.

Jack skirted the guard post, situated where the two lanes converged, and repeated his inspection along the other side, finding no more mines. Satisfied the road was clear, Jack made his way back to the truck to inspect the damage.

Paul interjected. "Might I posit that, although it appears the Germans wanted to ensure no one makes it *into* Luxembourg, *someone* intends to return to France."

It was a sobering observation.

Daniel joined Jack. "Major, I am so happy to see your concern for this piece of crap outweighs the health of your crew. Due warning next time."

"Unless you plan to give me a piggyback to Pétange, I'd recommend you stop flapping your lips and transfer your energies to jacking up the truck and changing the tyre."

Controlling the temptation to flip off his commanding officer, the sergeant did as he was told. Paul took pity on Daniel, and gave him a hand.

While the Morris was being repaired, Jack spread out the map on its hood. Evie joined him, the pair studying it with equal intensity.

"As far as I can tell we are about an hour away." Jack traced the jagged stretch of road between their current position and their destination.

Evie pulled the map closer to her, berating him for his decision not to follow the more direct route to Pétange. "If you had done as I said and driven north, we would be there by now."

"Highly doubtful, Evie. If we had, I guarantee we would be stuck outside Reims, hopscotching around US army trucks, and heading for more trouble than either of us can handle."

"Compared with four idiots about to face a battalion of German tanks?" Evie retorted.

"I still think we stand a better chance against a battalion of tanks, than the bulk of the Wehrmacht forces."

While neither Daniel nor Paul would ever qualify as pit crew at the Indianapolis Speedway, they *did* replace the tyre in decent time. The truck was ready to go before Jack came to check on their progress.

"Are you ladies done with your break? We have someplace to be before the war ends."

Not deigning to give Jack an obligatory chuckle, both men climbed into the truck bed, shooting the major matching glares of disapproval.

Disappointed he had failed to get a rise from either

Daniel or Paul, Jack kicked at the dirt like a child who had forgotten the punchline to a joke.

Circling around to the passenger side, he slumped into the seat next to Evie, who cast an annoyed glance at her traveling companion.

Paul nudged Daniel and smirked wickedly. "Perhaps he would have preferred us to roll the truck over him to prove our capabilities?"

The thought of their fearless leader being squished by the runaway Morris brought a howl of laughter from the enclosure.

Jack, on the other hand, straightened up in his seat, assuming they had finally understood his humour. He muttered smugly, "That's what I get for wasting highbrow wit on them."

The Morris drove on, unhindered by either German patrols or Luxembourg police.

The same could not be said for the Luxembourgian roads. The route between their crossing and Pétange was a sloppy mess. A combination of sleet and light snow resulted in their journey taking longer than Jack had hoped.

On more than one occasion, it required the efforts of the three passengers to free the sturdy little vehicle from an unavoidable quagmire.

It was late afternoon, and there was a welcome respite in the weather when the farm came into view. In excitement and fear, Evie elected to drive past the gate to the next rise.

Suspecting anyone or anything leaving the farm, would head in the direction they had just come from, Evie executed a skilful U-turn and parked the truck at the side of the road, partly hidden by the conveniently overhanging branches of a row of trees.

Jack hopped down and tapped on the side of the bed, instructing quietly, "Time to suit up, boys. We have a war to win."

Chapter Seventeen

15th December 1944
4:00 PM

The terrain leading to the farm was uneven, which, along with the sinuous shadows cast by the impending sunset, allowed the four to creep unseen to their target.

Each was armed with an M1 rifle and an American sidearm, as well as an ammo bag containing .30-06 cartridges and M9 anti-tank rockets.

The war had hardened Evie, physically. Had this been 1940, she would have struggled under the hefty load, in all likelihood compromising the success of the mission. Now, she found herself in second position and had, in fact, taken offence when Jack offered to carry her pack. Her crude gesture left him in no doubt of her pique.

Even had the load been more cumbersome than she was used to carrying, she was damned if she was going to admit it to the major.

They continued along an embankment until it became obvious the only viable direction was up.

Studying the angle of the slope, Evie whispered in Jack's ear, "Why would anybody choose a plot such as this to farm? Would it not be almost impossible to use a tractor?"

"Maybe it's not crops the Germans were planting here," Jack parried.

Spotting the telephone lines disappearing overhead, Jack pointed them out to Daniel, then waved his hand to the nearest pole.

Daniel nodded, patting Paul on the shoulder, signalling him to follow behind.

"Why send both?" Evie queried.

"Someone's gotta stand guard at the bottom to cover the good sergeant's rear while he's up there tapping into the line. Hope Hitler doesn't mind paying the long distance charges."

Jack and Evie watched Daniel begin to shimmy up the telephone pole. Safe in the knowledge Paul was at the ready to dissuade an inquisitive passer by, they ascended the steep slope.

Evie's astonishment when she discovered the top of the ridge had been levelled into a vast plateau was eclipsed by the sight of forty-five Panzerkampfwagen IV Ausführung H's parked neatly on the field.

It was so bizarre, she would not have been the slightest surprised to see a radio host preparing to broadcast some outlandish military game show devised by the German army to boost morale, with today's grand prize being a whole company of shiny new Panzers.

Jack had heard about the significant improvements the designers had put into this weapon over its predecessors. Thicker armour, coated with Zimmerit paste to prevent Allied magnetic anti-tank mines from adhering to the chassis, protected the crew inside. As for the tanks' firepower, they carried a potent 75-millimetre KwK40 L/48 gun, mounted to the turret.

While they were pretty to look at, Jack was concerned as to why they were sitting apparently unattended... and uncovered... where any idiot flying overhead should be able to spot them.

But no one in reconnaissance ever listened, did they? No matter how many times I tried to get their attention.

The touch of Evie's hand on his arm jerked Jack back to reality.

"Permit me to apologise for thinking you mad this entire time," she murmured, then, as though reading his thoughts, added, "Please tell me why they are parked like this?"

"For the life of me, Evie, I'm not completely certain." Jack's features scrunched in puzzlement. "I hope it is a conundrum we can solve."

Checking to make sure they were still alone, he scaled the tank. Soundlessly, he opened the hatch and crept inside.

Under the setting sun, the interior was black as night. Rifling through his pack for a torch, Jack's fingers found something cold and cylindrical, either the object of his search... or the shaft of an M9. Warily, he eased it from the pouch, relieved to see it was the former.

He switched it on, illuminating the corners of the compartment. The interior looked as immaculate as the exterior, with the exception of a few maps stacked in a neat pile.

Jack inspected each one, to discover they were merely roadmaps covering the area from their current position to Hanover, Germany.

Discarding them, Jack pointed the torch at the instrument panel, searching for and finding the fuel gauge.

Empty.

Mimicking the same ritual repeated by every motorist stranded at the side of the road, Jack tapped the glass expecting the needle to move. As history proved, it stayed obstinately on E.

Shining the light at the section which separated the fuel tanks from the cabin, Jack inched across to place his hand on the divider, feeling cold steel. Given the time of the year, this was not unexpected, but it *did* confirm this tank had been parked for more than a few days.

With the butt of the torch, he tapped the wall. In place of a muffled *plunk*, indicating they still had some fuel in them, he heard only the echo of drained tanks. Jack froze, afraid any Germans loitering in the vicinity had detected the sound as well.

He wasted precious seconds listening, but blessed silence regined.

Likewise, when he inspected the bin where the formidable main gun's projectiles were stored, he noted it too sat bare.

A beam of light broke through the open hatch, exacerbating Jack's fears. As he reached for his pistol, a thick Bronx accent asked, "Are you taking a nap in there or what?"

"Jesus, Fisher, I almost shot you," Jack admonished his sergeant in undertones.

"Wouldn't have been the first time somebody did. So what's the story?"

"Bone dry," Jack replied. "You and Paul check the next couple over."

As with the first, the scenario was identical in those tanks. Daniel and Paul confirmed Jack's suspicion when the four met up, crouching in the shadow of the great machines.

Paul jeered, "So now what, American? Your General Patton was correct all along. This was nothing more than a gamble by the Germans to distract your military intelligence from their main plans to the north.

"It is always the same with your ilk is it not, Donovon? You play your childish games of blind man's bluff. The Brits did it when they used Greece to cover the invasion of Sicily, your military did it using damn balloons in England to fool Hitler into thinking Calais was the objective on D-Day.

"And while you sit safely in your offices, congratulating each other on your ingenuity, and planning yet another deception, actual lives like my beautiful Henri's, are lost fighting the battles to cover your tracks."

Evie tried to calm Paul, adjuring, "Please, my friend, please hold it together."

Jack paid no attention to Paul's histrionics or Evie's efforts to placate the Frenchman, his concentration focused on deciphering the meaning of all of this.

"Why squander tanks this way?" he muttered. "They are in short supply in their armoury in the first place. Hell, our spies have told us the next generation of these goddamned metal boxes are stripped to the bone because of lack of parts. This battalion was the most decorated of all the tankers in the German army. They wouldn't just sideline these guys."

Daniel took the bull by the horns. "Major, I have to agree with Paul. It's time to admit you fuc— this was an exercise in futility, and get us the hell back to Paris before we get mixed—"

The drone of large engines firing up, snapped the quartet's scrutiny to a large barn adjacent to the main farmhouse.

Incredulous, the invaders watched as a man, dressed in an American uniform, pushed open the barn's door, revealing the masked headlights of a Studebaker US6 6x6 truck. The vehicle drove out onto the gravel, heading to the main road.

Jack spotted the familiar white star painted on the olive-drab door, as it passed.

Four more similarly adorned two-and-a-half-ton trucks paraded out of the building. The last one paused long enough for the soldier who had been waiting by the door to climb into the back, hands reaching out to haul him inside.

The chains on the rear tires jangled in a steady rhythm as it caught up with the rest.

"Sacré bleu," Paul cried. "What game are you Americans playing?"

Dumbfounded, Jack was caught off guard. "No… this can't be. There's not supposed to be any troop movement in Luxembourg yet—"

He was interrupted by the throaty growl of a US army issue WLA motorbike. Its headlight indicated it was also preparing to depart the confines of the barn.

In the instant the rider was silhouetted in the glow from the building's illumination, Evie abandoned her concern for Paul, and dropped to her stomach. Taking aim at the man's shoulder, she determined it was time for answers.

The crack of her M1, resonated instantaneously with the sound of a second.

Her bullet ripped through the rider's flesh, knocking him off balance, while Jack's obliterated the stolen WLA's front tyre.

Bike and rider spun, throwing up mud and stone chips as both ground into the dirt.

Anxious to bag their quarry before it could untangle itself from the wrecked motorcycle, Evie and Jack charged.

Daniel glanced at Paul. Anger at the pair's reckless disregard for their own safety burned within his gaze. All the same, he pelted after them.

As for Paul, he was torn between leaving the lot and avenging Henri's honour.

Still struggling with his decision, he caught the remnants of the December sun disappearing below the horizon. Nostalgia touched his heart.

Henri always favoured this time of the day, though he never told me why.

Somehow, it helped make up his mind. Rising to his feet, Paul hurried to catch the others.

He joined the trio who had circled the bleeding man dressed in an American army captain's uniform. Watching their captive rise awkwardly to his knees and attempt to lock his fingers behind his head, Paul studied his face.

Even masked by his goggles, there was something familiar about him.

Evie already knew.

The man might have dyed his hair black in a feeble effort to disguise himself, but when Evie wrenched off his goggles, she exposed the snarling glare of Johan Kristiansen.

Chapter Eighteen

4:50 PM

Pain lanced through Kristiansen's shoulder when Daniel and Jack hoisted his arms above his head, the rope biting into his wrists as it was pulled taut around the rafter.

Watching the Norwegian struggle to dance on the toes of his polished boots, Jack was confident their hostage was not going anywhere quickly. He patted Daniel on the shoulder, and asked him to secure the other end of the rope to one of the stalls.

Jack pulled up a milk stool next to the twirling man who spat obscenities at Daniel. "Unbind me, cur before I free myself and feed you to the pigs."

"Johan, Johan, I am sure your mother raised you to be more respectful than that," Jack chided.

"Shut your mouth about my mother," Kristiansen ordered hotly. "You know nothing about her."

"You're right," Jack agreed. "Only the bits I've read about how she was left to the mercy of your neighbours after you opted for a better life sucking off the teat…" he could not help but chuckle at the accidental irony of his statement considering Kristiansen was strung up from a barn rafter like a freshly gutted hog. "...of your Uncle Adolf.

"My sources tell me she's eking out a meagre living by taking in laundry and whoring out your siblings to the local German garrison..." Jack paused to rub his chin. "...'though I could be misinformed about your sisters. It might just be anyone willing to spend 10 Reichspfennig on them."

"I told you to shut your damn mouth," Kristiansen hissed. "You know nothing about my family, American."

"More than you might think, Johan. Take your father for instance. You remember your father, don't you? How could you forget the man you sacrificed for the sake of your advancement. Nice touch accusing him of being a member of the resistance."

Growing impatient with Jack's idle mockery, Evie pushed past him to shove the barrel of her rifle into Kristiansen's stomach. Memories of the atrocities perpetrated by this man against not only the citizens of Paris, but all of France, overwhelmed her.

"Enough, Jack. Let us execute him here and now, and be on our way. He is not worth our time."

With a disdainful laugh, Kristiansen sneered, "Woman, you do not have the nerve to do that. Like all the rabbits in your Godforsaken country you are little more than bluster.

"Your mighty French army outnumbers the glorious Third Reich in not only the numbers of tanks and troops but also, technology. As ever, when push came to shove, France folded like the proverbial deck of cards because there was nobody talented enough to lead."

With a cruel grin, he taunted, "How did your husband... Claude I believe his name was... fare, Madam Rousseau? Oh, yes they sacrificed him in Calais to save their collective backsides."

Hearing her beloved's name on the vile lips of this despicable creature, Evie gaped, slacked-jawed. The white hot fury which exploded within her obliterated the fact that somehow, he knew her identity.

Without thinking, she disengaged the safety on her rifle and cocked the hammer back. "Die, you bastard."

Evie did not see Jack leap to his feet to nudge the barrel away from Kristiansen's gut. The bullet still lacerated the Norwegian's side, leaving a bloody trail on his stolen uniform.

Daniel, who had been snooping through the rear of the barn, dove for cover, barely avoiding the stray bullet which buried itself into the post next to where he had been standing.

"Jesus Christ," he shouted, which elicited an evil cackle from Kristiansen.

"Praying won't save your sorry hide, cur."

Flipping her rifle around, Evie jabbed the butt into Kristiansen's wound. "Shut your fucking mouth, you murderous—"

Jack grabbed her by the shoulders, separating the pair. Spinning her to face him, he tried to appeal to her normally reasonable conscience.

"Evie, listen to me…"

"No, Jack, that rabid wolf needs to be put down… please let me."

"Evie, stop and think… you refer to him as the Wolf but, from what I see, he is nothing more than a mangy mongrel. You've muzzled him… torn his venomous fangs from his jaws. Beyond that, he has divulged vital information without saying a word."

This penetrated Evie's fury and, arching a curious eyebrow, she glanced over her shoulder.

"Do not believe the American's shit, woman, I have told you nothing."

Jack's implacable gaze bore into Kristiansen. "Is that so, Johan? How about we start with your choice of dress? Now, I understand the caravan which left you here. Afraid to face the action yourself?" he scoffed.

"Nein," Kristiansen roared.

"Enough of your feeble endeavours at being a German, boy," Jack rebuked. "I daresay Sergeant Fisher possesses more German heritage than you."

"None that I would claim," Daniel defended himself

Paying no heed to Daniel's remark, Jack listed the facts of life, their captive now faced. "I suspect you realise, Kristiansen, that in your current uniform, you are regarded as a spy and can be legally interrogated and hanged as one.

"Keep that in mind, you worthless piece of shit, because I am going to ask you two questions to which you will answer promptly and comprehensively.

"And let me reassure you, if I doubt the veracity of anything you say, I will leave this barn and allow my two friends here from the French Resistance..." Jack pulled his Bowie knife from its sheath on his belt, and handed it to Evie. "...to deal with you as they see fit."

In his arrogance, Kristiansen had forgotten about the American uniform, not to mention the ramifications of being found wearing it. Still, he had played the hardened villain since 1940, and he was not about to exhibit any sign of fear to these losers.

He bragged, "I am a Standartenführer in the Führer's Schutzstaffel. Your threats mean nothing to me. Go ahead, do your best. I have broken stronger men than the lot of you combined before breakfast."

Jack shook his head and, stepping alongside the hanging Norwegian, warned in a low voice, "If I find you are not forthcoming, you will only have yourself to blame for your death. I guarantee you, the woman behind me will make sure you regret that I did not allow her to take your life quickly when she had the opportunity."

Kristiansen spat in Jack's face, which did not faze the latter, who wiped the spittle with the back of his hand and smeared it on Kristiansen's jacket.

"Shall we begin, Standartenführer Kristiansen? Where are those trucks heading?"

"Do you honestly believe I will capitulate so readily? You are a fool."

"Nope, can't say I did." Moving to one side, Jack nodded at Evie. "Madame Rousseau, feel free to flay your pound of flesh. I suggest starting along the nice crease you left on his side. He will peel more easily."

Evie could not believe her ears. Jack had just prevented her from shooting the bastard, and now he was giving her the go ahead to cut Kristiansen open. The remains of her conscience screamed that this was not something she had the stomach to do.

Her expressionless façade masked her inner turmoil. She took two steps, lifting the knife to the still bleeding wound, and purposely allowing the polished steel of the blade to reflect the light in the barn.

In vain, Kristiansen struggled to match the woman's resolve, but when the glint caught his eye, he cracked.

SS officer Johan Kristiansen was not the one holding the knife this time. He had no desire to suffer the same horrors he had inflicted on his unfortunate victims.

Perhaps Choltitz was right all along, Kristiansen's brain contended. *There is no cause worth sacrificing one's life.*

Feeling the tug as Evie sliced open his jacket, he yelled, "For the love of God, stop."

He had heard this plea from many a man, followed by the

bubbling of snot filled tears when he refused to heed their request. Torture had been his one true release. To him it was an aphrodisiac, more potent than whatever drug Hitler might be ingesting at any given moment.

Jack placed a hand on Evie's arm, halting her.

Turning her back on the Norwegian, Evie dropped the blade onto the hay strewn floor beneath him. Without a word, she walked to the door and let the cold wind embrace her.

"I will ask you one last time. Where are those trucks heading?"

"R-Reims," Kristiansen stammered, then fell silent remembering he had not played the last of his cards. The smile returned to his lips, *there is still a way to emerge from this, relatively unscathed.*

"American, you have a choice. What is more important to you? Saving the lives of an untold number of Allied soldiers about to face the bulk of the remaining Wehrmacht's Western forces or becoming the true *Saviour of Paris* instead of that coward Choltitz?"

"Paris? We both know that is bullshit, Kristiansen," Jack argued. "Whatever lunatic plan Adolf might have hatched, died with those empty tanks outside."

"You have such a limited imagination, American," Kristiansen's grin widened. "Do you honestly think, even if a fully-fledged battle is taking place in the Ardennes, nobody would notice a column of *German* tanks heading to the seat of French cowardice?"

"Exactly," Jack countered. "Which means you are merely stalling for the time your men need to evade capture."

"You might be right... *or* there might be forty-five *acquired* French tanks, with enough petrol and ammunition waiting for them in Reims to level the streets of that putrid city."

He laughed manically.

"Or…" Kristiansen dangled the juiciest prize, one he assumed the American major would not be able to pass up.

"Or?"

"Or would you rather be the *Saviour of All Europe* and seize the submarine readying to depart from the pens in…"

"Enough of your games. Just explain the importance of this vessel, which I have no doubt the British Navy will sink before it reaches the open sea," Jack retorted, rebuffing Kristiansen's belief that the sub stood any chance of securing a safe harbour, save the bottom of the Atlantic.

"Release me, and I will tell you."

"Convince me of the worth of your intelligence first."

"Let me just say, if that submarine makes it out of German waters, all the lives lost in the Allied push to reach Berlin will be for naught."

Chapter Nineteen

5:35 PM

The guttural thrum of an engine coming from the rear of the barn captured everyone's attention.

Instinctively, Jack gripped his forty-five, unsure whether the source of the noise meant they had unexpected company.

Appearing from the depths of a stall, the shit-eating grin on Sergeant Fisher's face outshone Kristiansen's contemptuous one.

"Sorry to interrupt, Major." Daniel appeared, wiping his hand on a rag. "Seems the Germans, in their hurry to make it to their appointment, left us one of their Studebakers as a gift, and looks in a lot better shape than the pile of crap we left under those trees. Full tank of gas, all-terrain vehicle."

He sounded more like a car salesman than a soldier. "It'll get us there without turning our bones to soup."

Jack raised his hand to arrest the used car spiel before Daniel could ask whether he wanted undercoating to go with it, "How on earth did you come across such a rare find, Sergeant Fisher?"

"Apparently, one of those Nazi super idiots was too clumsy to turn a simple key, and it snapped in the ignition. Guess none of them tried to boost their girlfriend's dad's car to take her on a joyride. Don't they teach those geniuses how to hotwire a vehicle? Anyway, I figured you might be done with this putz, and would want to be on the road to intercept the convoy heading to Reims."

It appeared Sergeant Daniel Fisher had made the executive decision as to their next destination.

"By all means, Sergeant. Is there a way out back there?"

The exit via front of the building, blocked by a certain suspended Norwegian.

"Aye, Major," Daniel replied, then asked Paul. "Care to help me open it?"

Paul nodded and accompanied Daniel to the rear of the barn. The pair pushed hard on the old door; the jarring screech of the rusty rollers set everyone's teeth on edge.

Returning to the truck, Daniel climbed into the driver's side, refusing to be relegated to the bed of the vehicle. Likewise, Paul claimed the passenger seat.

Jack stooped to retrieve his knife.

Relief swept through Kristiansen, sure the American would indeed cut him down and liberate him, based on the minimal but enlightening information he had provided.

As long as this fool gives me enough time to make it back to Norway. Kristiansen made some quick calculations as to how he could save his hide. *I will head north and disappear into Lapland.*

His hope of clemency was short-lived.

Kristiansen's sense of foreboding intensified as the major rose to his feet, sheathed his blade, and brushed hay off his trousers, before walking past the SS officer without so much as an acknowledgement.

Renewed fear of abandonment welled within Kristiansen.

Frantically, he tried to pirouette on his toes, preparing to demand the American honour his agreement to free him.

Before the words left his mouth, the major spun on his heel.

Rather than addressing the trussed enemy officer dressed in a US army uniform, Jack looked at Evie. "We'll meet you at the front. Please make sure to close the door behind you. We don't want Johan to catch a chill."

Kristiansen twisted around to see Evie incline her head in agreement.

In silence, Evie watched the large truck drive out of the stall and disappear through the rear door, which Jack managed to haul almost closed as he followed.

Before taking her leave, she retraced her steps to Kristiansen, and pinned him with fury-filled eyes.

"Release me. You cannot leave me here to freeze to death," he ordered, clearly forgetting he was in no position to issue instructions.

Patting the Norwegian's pockets, Evie discovered a pack of American cigarettes and a lighter. She tapped one out, placed it between her lips and lit it.

The end of the cigarette glowed as she inhaled slowly.

"You heard the major. He wants me to close the door on my way out, to ensure you do not succumb to the cold."

She walked to the open door, Kristiansen's curses ringing in her ears.

"I will see you hunted down, bitch," he promised. "I will make sure justice sends you to hell for this barbaric cruelty. You will know no peace. I shall see you suffer like your worthless soldier of a husband."

Goaded, Evie swivelled to face him.

Exercising all her self-discipline, she composed herself and, in a voice devoid of emotion, said, "You are right, Standartenführer Kristiansen, it would be remiss of me to leave you this way. Almost as inhuman as what you and your friends did to the citizens of Oradour-sur-Glane. You remember that village, yes?

"It was very civilised of you all to see that the women and children were ushered into their church so they could pray to God. I guess herding their husbands into the barns away from their loved ones was to make sure the men would not interrupt?"

She took a final drag of the cigarette, before forcing the man to relive the atrocity he had committed.

"Can you hear them, Kristiansen? Can you hear them pleading to God for mercy as you set them and their entire village on fire?"

Evie flipped open the lighter, bringing the flame to life one last time. She threw it into the pile of hay littering the floor of the stall where the rope was tied off, then discarded the burning cigarette on the straw at his feet.

Watching both piles ignite almost simultaneously, Evie strode out, spying the headlights of the truck rounding the corner of the barn.

Pulling the great door shut, she suggested with exaggerated politeness, "If I were you, you bastard, I would pray as loudly as possible that God allows the rope to burn through before the fire at your feet claims your worthless hide."

The bang of the wood against its frame, muffled Kristiansen's screams of excruciating pain.

As Evie clambered into the back of the truck, Jack heard an agonised and somewhat disembodied shriek but was unsure from where, exactly, it originated, or even whether it was human.

"What was that?"

"Poor Johan took offence to my advice that he ought to give up smoking."

The Studebaker made it halfway down the drive, aiming for the spot where Daniel had left the field phone when the barn erupted into a fireball. Flames engulfed its wooden framework... and everything inside.

In Evie's desire to mete out justice to the man being immolated, she had not given a second's thought as to whether any of the trucks, which previously occupied the building had developed a fuel leak.

The rapid acceleration of the fire alerted her to a definitive error in judgment. Apparently, at least one of the vehicles they were in pursuit of was indeed defective and could well be capable of slowing the rest down along the way.

Hearing the roar of the inferno, Daniel stomped on the brakes. He and Paul leapt out of the cab to see what was happening. Jack poked his head through the canvas flaps at the rear.

Glancing at Evie, he saw her remove a packet of cigarettes from her pocket and calmly slide one out.

"Do you have a light, Jack? I seem to have mislaid mine."

Jack stretched out his arm and flicked the lid of his black and silver Ronson Tuxedo Lighter, a gift from his father on the day he enlisted.

Jack gave his old man credit for prepping the younger Donovon to be ready for the day when a beautiful woman would depend on his generosity to escape a problematic situation.

His dad had inscribed on the silver plate: *Never question why, nor refuse.*

The flame touched the tip of Evie's cigarette which flared red, as she drew the smoke deep into her lungs. She held it there briefly, picturing the Norwegian struggling for his last breath, then allowed it to escape on a sigh. The smoke formed a jagged halo above her head.

"I should listen to my own advice and give up this habit, they could be the death of a person," she said cynically

Taking a last puff before crushing it out on the bed of the truck, Evie peered at the two men captivated by the intensity of the fire. Embers had blown to an adjacent tree, igniting the dead leaves clinging to it. Paul was positive the house would suffer the same fate.

"Sergeant Fisher," she cooed. "Might you and Paul see fit to climb back in the cab and catch up to our prey. I think one of their vehicles might already be crippled."

"B-but what about contacting Paris to let them know?" Daniel queried as he settled behind the wheel.

"No, time for that, Sergeant," Evie told him flatly.

"I risked my ass climbing up there," Daniel protested.

"We can do that in Reims if you stop arguing with me and get your precious ass moving."

"Sergeant," Jack broke in. "You heard the woman. Besides, we cannot be sure who will answer the other end of the field phone or how many faceless bureaucrats posing as soldiers we will get passed through. I happen to have de Gaulle's office number."

"A man who loves you so much, Major, he's sure to be waiting to hear from you with bated breath," Daniel retorted.

"Road. Now. Fisher," Jack commanded.

Daniel grimaced at Paul. "Him I can take, but how did you put up with her for so long?"

"By never questioning her decisions, my friend."

Chapter Twenty

11:20 PM

The drizzle had returned in earnest, and the cold front sweeping in with the night, brought the odd snow flurry dancing in front of the headlights, clinging to the windscreen.

In addition to the weather, the chains used by the Germans were hindering their progress. The convoy chugged along at a speed well below the customary thirty miles an hour.

All this proved beneficial to the band chasing them.

The muddy ruts left by the chained-lashed tyres on the German fleet were freezing with every passing minute. This meant the likelihood of the 6x6 driven by Sergeant Fisher getting stuck in some puddle was lessening gradually and, free of the troublesome snow chains, they had the added advantage of speed.

Regrettably, although the Studebaker could reach forty-five, flat out, current conditions severely limited its normal pace. Neither did they make the ride any smoother. The large truck jarred its passengers' bones with each bounce.

"Christ, Fisher," Jack complained through the rear window. "Can you get us there in one piece and not kill us before we have a crack at the tankers?"

"I'm trying my best, Major. But if you want to bitch at anybody about the lousey roads, might I suggest you address your complaint to Luxembourg's National Roads Administration."

Easing around a curve, close to the border they had crossed earlier in the day, the truck's headlights flashed off something red just ahead on the French side.

Drawing alongside, Daniel and Paul recognised it as one of the Studebakers, hastily abandoned. They got out to inspect the vehicle.

When Daniel climbed into the cab, he noticed the gas gauge, which told him the truck was as empty of fuel as the worthless collection of tanks at the farm. "I'll be damned. She was right."

Through the windscreen, he saw Paul clamber onto the truck's bumper and place his hand on the hood.

"I do not think they are more than a half hour ahead of us," Paul observed. "These treacherous roads and the weight of all those extra bodies has slowed them down."

"Yeah, and it looks like they didn't have Triple A membership to ring for help." Daniel chuckled.

"Triple what?" Paul raised a quizzical brow, having no idea what the American found so funny.

"Never mind, Paul," Daniel grunted. "Why don't you check in the back to see whether they left us any goodies, instead of killing my jokes."

140

While Daniel and Paul combed through the stricken Studebaker, discussing the distance between themselves and the other three trucks, Jack decided to take advantage of the pause. Jumping down from their vehicle, he sloshed back along the road to the deserted French border-guard shack.

Testing the knob, he found the door still locked. Snatching a convenient rock, Jack hurled it through the glass, sending splinters across the wooden floor.

Easing his arm through the hole where the pane had been, his fingers found the lock under the doorknob. Biting his tongue, he toyed with the latch until the lock sprang free. Pistol in hand, Jack pushed open the door and crept inside.

A useless toggle of the light switch told him the electricity had been cut to the small building. With no alternative, Jack pulled his torch from his belt, and clicked it on, the narrow beam swallowed in the darkness

Motionless, he waited for his eyes to adjust.

The first thing the light exposed was a dark stain on one of the desks. A flash to the other desk revealed a matching stain in the middle of the battered surface.

Licking his fingers to warm them, Jack swiped one through the stain to confirm it was not coffee. The frozen mess melted at his touch. Examining the fluid under the flashlight, Jack knew it was blood.

"I doubt they even saw it coming," Jack murmured to the vacant office.

As though trying to obliterate the image in his mind of the senseless deaths which had occurred in this dilapidated guard house, Jack wiped his fingers on his pants, to rid them of the blood.

The arc of his flashlight illuminated the office phone splayed across the floor. Jack grimaced at the condition of the machine. A tangle of wire remained from where it had been wrenched off the wall. "Dammit."

"Did you think…"

Startled, Jack spun around to see Evie standing in the doorway, arms folded.

"…to check whether the connection to the pole outside is still live?"

Before he could answer, she edged past him to look out of the window. A smile twitched her lips. In their haste, the Germans had neither cut down the pole, nor removed the main line. Only the line linking the shack to the pole had been severed.

Gathering the discarded phone, Evie headed outside to the dangling telephone wire. Hearing Jack behind her, she ordered, "Knife."

Jack placed it in her waiting palm and watched her strip the main wire and re-attach the remains of the phone wire hanging from the handset, with the speed and skill of an expert.

With a flip of the blade, Evie presented the handle to Jack, then tapped the telephone's cradle a couple of times, bringing the phone to life.

Gingerly, she handed it to Jack, quipping, "Make sure to deposit the correct amount for the next three minutes."

The man on the receiving end of the annoyingly ringing phone was anything but pleased to be disturbed at this time of night. Mattheu Garnier had just managed to close his eyes for the first time in the last thirty-six hours.

He could not refuse the call. His position as de Gaulle's aide-de-camp meant it could be anybody from a general in the middle of a pitched battle, to Roosevelt sitting by his insipid fireplace, preparing to offer encouraging words to the new leader of France.

Lifting the receiver, he answered tersely, "Colonel Garnier speaking."

The American accent which greeted him sent a chill down his spine, even more than the caller's ease of using his first name.

"Thank God you're still up, Mattheu. Please put me through to the general immediately."

"First, *Major Donovon*, need I remind you *again* to address me with the proper military respect. Secondly, the General has retired for the evening."

Jack and Mattheu had met when Jack was an aspiring attaché to a long retired and ailing general. He had been required to accompany the addle-minded genius to Paris and Berlin in the guise of a military observer in the early thirties.

His *actual* duty during that mission was to ensure the general did not accidentally say something which would result in a live-fire war.

Mattheu, on the other hand, was a brash artillery commander with a penchant for heavy drinking and gambling. The two had hit it off immediately.

"I can guarantee he has no intention of speak—"

"He will when you tell him I was right all along. The Germans are—"

"Listen, Jackson." Mattheu tried to maintain his composure. "The General has no desire to listen to your blathering insanity about some secret tank command. You do not know how much damage me standing up for you has done to my reputation. The General contemplated replacing me, especially when he discovered both Eisenhower and Patton had sent you packing."

"Mattheu, just shut up and listen to—"

"No, my friend, *you* listen for once. We have enough to worry about. The 2nd Panzer Division has been seen heading west towards Belgium."

"I understand your situation, Colonel. But whatever hell is about to break up there is nothing compared with what is coming your way."

"Fine, Major Donovon," Mattheu replied, exasperated with Jack's refusal to take *no* for an answer. "Give me the details, and I will see it is passed along official channels."

Jack sighed. He knew the term *official channels* meant de Gaulle would never see the message.

Jack's infuriated expression informed Evie the conversation was not going as planned. Seeing him preparing to plead his case a final time, sparked her own anger.

With the speed of a striking cobra, Evie snatched the receiver. The precariously wired connection crackled and threatened to disconnect in the process.

Not caring who or what rank the person on the other end held, she yelled, "Monsieur, you can either get that lazy bâtard, de Gaulle, out of bed and tell him a brigade of our Somua tanks manned by German tankers are heading for the heart of Paris to finish the job Choltitz refused to carry out, or you can wait until he is greeted with a SA 35 gun shoved up his ridiculously huge nose. Either way, he needs to order Leclerc and his armoured units to Reims before…"

Evie stopped speaking and canted her head, listening intently, then removed the receiver from her ear, studied it quizzically, and lifted her gaze to Jack.

"What did Mattheu say?"

"He mumbled something about crazy Americans and hung up."

"Do you think he took you seriously?"

"Who can tell with the French Military." Evie shrugged.

Jack was tempted to ring back, but Evie snapped the connection and cast the remains of the phone into the mounting slush.

"If they are not going to help, Jack, it is up to us to save the city."

The crunch of footfalls curbed Jack's tongue. It was obvious Evie had made up her mind.

"If you two are done sending out seasonal greetings to the Gestapo, you might want to take a gander at what we found." Paul invited.

Without discussion the three retraced their steps to find Daniel busily securing a crate in the bed of their truck.

"What have you got there, Sergeant Fisher?" Jack asked.

"A most thoughtful Hanukkah present, Boss." Daniel chuckled. "The Germans left us a case of Panzerfaust anti-tank rockets. Generous of them don'tcha think?"

"Now, now, Sergeant. I'm sure it was a simple oversight on their part. We better get going so we can return them by airmail.

Chapter Twenty-One

Outside Reims, France
16th December 1944
2:18 AM

The lead vehicle of the remaining camouflaged trucks reached the outskirts of Reims about ten minutes ahead of the other three.

In the passenger seat of the Studebaker, Oberst Friedrich König fumed. Not only were they running behind schedule, but also they were on the cusp of jeopardising the entire mission.

His irritation was compounded by having to dress in a US Colonel's uniform, rather than his beloved German greys. He did not care that the order to do so had come from Hitler himself.

Secretly, König believed the Führer's meddling in matters of war preparation had long since cost Germany the victory as surely as had Kaiser Wilhelm's in the Great War.

He held both men in contempt for betraying the Fatherland in exchange for personal gain.

König reached under the coat to scratch his chest raw.

"Our quality uniforms would never chafe like this," he complained aloud.

"Did you say something, Oberst?" queried the young man dressed as a corporal.

"Just keep your eyes on the road and your mouth shut."

The corporal fell silent until he discerned a set of headlights facing them through the snow flurries.

"Ober—"

"English, dunderhead. Do you want to get us all killed? Just say the word and I'll start with you."

The corporal's trembling hand released the wheel and pointed at the unexpected company. "Do I drive through them?"

Sighing, König shook his head. "No, you fool, pull over."

Before the sergeant alighted from his jeep, he said to the man standing behind the fifty calibre Browning, "Harrison, keep your gun trained on the driver. If he sneezes in German, open fire."

Private William Henry Harrison stared at his superior officer.

Wanting to clarify the order, he asked, "What does a German sneeze sound like, Sarge?"

"For Christ's sake, Harrison, just make sure you're ready to fire that thing.

"Carmichael..." he said in a hushed tone to his corporal who had been busy trying to stay warm in the passenger seat, "...get on the horn to HQ and find out why we have traffic here tonight?"

"Will do, Sarge."

Carmichael wound the crank on the field phone, and waited for Sparky on the other end to answer.

Deciding that to wait for the sergeant to approach the truck and carry on a conversation with the numskull in the driver's seat was not a risk worth taking, König climbed out.

He tapped quietly on the side of the bed to warn those in the back to stand ready.

At the driver's side door, he met the sergeant who saluted. "Evening, Colonel."

König returned the salute and greeted the man, cordially.

"Evening, Sergeant…" König dragged out the man's rank to get the soldier to introduce himself.

"Deavers, Colonel. Sergeant Charles Deavers, Third Army."

"Nice to make your acquaintance, Sergeant Deavers," König replied, reaching for his pack of American unfiltered smokes. Tapping the pack, he tilted it towards Deavers.

Knowing better than to refuse one from a commanding officer, the sergeant accepted both the cigarette and a light.

As he puffed the cigarette to life, Deavers asked, "What brings you out on this frigid night, Colonel…" Deavers played König's game as well.

"Colonel Alexander Bishop, 29th ID out of Fort Belvoir, Virginia."

"Guards, huh?" Deavers asked, with a hint of condescension. His own platoon was thick with National Guard units. In his opinion, none of their training was up to snuff.

"Aye, Sergeant. Working hand in hand with HQ since *Normandy*." The fake colonel said, emphasising his supposed unit's merit in the Normandy invasion.

Preferring not to get mired in a pissing contest, König

chose a different tack. "Sure is a bitch of a night isn't it, Sergeant Deavers?"

During the period of König's life that no one in the world could account for, he had bounced back and forth between England and the United States, serving his country as a military spy. In doing so, he had sharpened his American accent and learned their idiosyncrasies.

A faint and inexplicable niggle of unease pestering his subconscious, the sergeant chanced a reprimand to press, "That it is, Colonel, but shouldn't you and your men be heading north for the party?"

Shoving his hands into his pants' pockets, König feigned frustration. "If only. Seems the geniuses at HQ reckon our skills are better put to use playing traffic cops in Reims."

"Beggin' your pardon, Colonel Bishop. We've been here since eighteen hundred hours and nobody notified us of any guard change. Are you sure your orders are—"

"Sergeant Deavers, may I speak with you for a sec?" Carmichael sang out. He did not elaborate, only held out the field phone.

Ice slunk down Deavers' spine. In the time he had served with Carmichael, the corporal had never addressed him as anything other than *Sarge*. The switch was a sure sign something was up.

"If you will excuse me for a moment, Colonel, that's probably them right now. Late as always." The sergeant smiled politely.

König heard the rumble of the other trucks. He glanced over his shoulder and caught the gleam of headlights reflected in the rifle barrels of his men standing at the ready alongside the vehicle. "By all means, Sergeant." König nodded.

As Deavers turned, König opened the flap of his .45 holster. "By the way, Sergeant Deavers, there's rumours about Germans joyriding through the countryside posing as American soldiers. Who won the last World Series?"

The Americans are so predictable, König thought as he waited for the answer, *believing no one else on the planet was smart enough to read a paper about American sports.*

Deavers stopped in his tracks and chuckled, "If you could call it an actual Series, the Redbirds beat the Browns in six."

The bullet from König's Colt tore through the sergeant's back and out of his chest, as his men opened a relentless salvo on the jeep.

Private Harrison was hit multiple times before he could return fire in the direction of the attack. A spasm in his fingers, when death claimed him, caused them to lock around the trigger of the gun, unleashing a burst of fifty calibre cartridges.

As he and the gun slumped to the right, Carmichael was riddled with bullets before he could avoid them, his lifeless body thrown against the jeep's dash.

König waved at his men to cease fire. His pistol still drawn, he walked to the sergeant's body. He shook his head, disappointed with himself for not killing Deavers with one shot.

Maybe it is time to retire, König mused.

He stood over the dying man and, with the toe of his boot, tipped the soldier onto his back. A cruel smile caused the lines around his eyes to crinkle maliciously.

"Danke sehr, Sergeant Deavers, for aiding the Fatherland with your invaluable baseball update."

A single bullet hit the American in the forehead.

"I'm sure I will find use for it sometime today," König said smugly, holstering his gun.

Spinning on his heel, he ordered the occupants in the newly arriving vehicles, "Bewegen Sie diesen verdammten

Jeep und seien Sie schnell dabei." (Move this damn jeep and be quick about it.)

His men scurried to carry out the Oberst's orders. While three dragged the bodies of the dead soldiers to a ditch, four others pushed the jeep off the road.

Cresting the hill a few hundred feet behind the caravan, Daniel doused the truck's lights, hoping no one below had spotted them, praying the sound of their engine went unnoticed among the drone of the other Studebakers ahead.

Hearing the commotion, Evie hopped down from the vehicle, much to Jack's annoyance.

"Goddammit, Evie, get back here. I don't need you getting killed doing something stupid."

"Shut up, Major and hand me a Panzerfaust out of that case. I'm going to let these bastards know they have run out of time."

"No, Evie, I—"

"Now, Jack Donovon!"

Jack grumbled under his breath about the lunacy of whatever she had in mind, but it was apparent he was not going to stop her. If he refused her request she would doubtless climb back in to take it herself.

He lowered it to her, carefully. Evie struggled with the weight as she crouched into a kneeling position. This rocket felt heavier than the ones she had used previously. Flipping up the sight, she found it had been improved as well, thinking, *this cannot be a 30. It is at least twice as heavy, must be one of the 100's we heard the Germans were testing.*

Adjusting to the upgraded weapon, Evie sighted the last truck, watching the soldiers scrambling into the vehicle. Inhaling, she held her breath and pulled the trigger.

The projectile lit the barrel as it rushed down range. Spots danced in Evie's eyes, and she was positive she had missed her target completely until a spectacular explosion boomed into the night. In an instant, the truck was reduced to a fiery silhouette against the darkness as flames devoured it, blazing figures jumping for their lives into snowy ditches.

A secondary eruption from the munitions stored in the bed of the truck, propelled the vehicle about six feet skywards before dumping it on its side on top of those rushing to escape.

The blast launched a fireball forwards, igniting the canvas of the third truck. Men inside scrabbled to rip off the tarp before they suffered the same fate as those behind them.

Unsure who or where the attackers were, König raced to his truck, fleeing before he could be targeted. He did not give a damn whether any of those accompanying him were injured or dead. His own safety was his primary concern.

Seeing the lead truck take off, the two surviving transporters fell in line.

While Evie had thinned the herd of tankers set to attack Paris, she had caused another problem.

The flaming debris from the decimated Studebaker was scattered haphazardly across the road, delaying Daniel's ability to give chase. That and drawing indiscriminate rifle fire from the last vehicle in the convoy as the Germans escaped.

Chapter Twenty-Two

3:00 AM

E vie's fireworks resulted in a cacophony of ancient church bells, saved from the German blast furnaces by the residents of Reims, clanging throughout the town to summon their men to action.

People awoke fearful the Germans were rampaging their town once more. Local volunteer firefighters, along with the town's militia, raced to the source of the commotion.

The confusion masked the travels of three army lorries which were somewhere they were not supposed to be.

König's truck arrived at the massive one-time grain processing centre. Even before the engine was cut, he had directed the soldiers out into formation.

An order repeated when the other two vehicles drew up, shortly thereafter. Moving along the assembled ranks, König took an inventory of his men.

Ninety-seven... ninety-eight... ninety-nine... scheisse, only one hundred, he thought angrily.

Out of the 145 with whom he had left Pétange, sufficient to outfit the forty-five French Somua S35 tanks he was assigned, König was down to barely enough three-men teams to operate thirty-three — thanks to the cowardly assassin who had attacked them in the dark.

Why didn't that errand boy, Kristiansen, stick around to take part? He would have been helpful enough to load the gun... or be cannon fodder.

As König marched to the front of the lines, he affixed a stern countenance upon his face, and silently pledged vengeance for the loss of his courageous soldiers. *I will see one hundred Parisians are slain for each of you.*

Clasping his hands behind his back, he rocked on his heels, savouring the attention he commanded from the men before him.

Finally, he spoke, "Gentlemen, unlike Herr Goebbels, I have no rousing speech calculated to stir your pride for the Fatherland..."

The slight was directed at the Reich Minister of Propaganda, Joseph Goebbels, and his impassioned, yet unnecessarily long-winded, speeches on Aryan dogma. His words drew a chuckle from the assemblage.

König thought Goebbels, along with the vast majority of the Nazi regime, had been duped into accepting the ludicrously misguided concept that they belonged to the so-called Aryan race, and why... given the true origins of the term dated back to ancient India and Iran... *any* in the party's hierarchy would claim to be a descendant.

He classed them as lazy, self-entitled bureaucrats, more

interested in parading around in their designer uniforms and stealing the wealth of Europe than winning the war.

"...and also, unlike Herr Goebbels, I know the true metal within each of you, and your steadfast valour as German soldiers.

"What we are tasked to do shortly will not only demonstrate that to the rest of the world, but will also, beyond a doubt, affect the future for centuries to come.

"We shall be like the Valkyries of legend, and smite our foes. We will advance on Paris and reduce it to smouldering embers."

Instead of offering up the Party's salute and customary *Heil Hitler*, König brought his clenched right fist to his heart, shouting in what he hoped was old Norse, "Heill til þú!" (Hail to you) in respect for his men.

Concern swept through the ranks at this seditious refusal to acknowledge the Führer as they had been taught to do since childhood.

Maintaining his salute to them, König observed, "Our glorious Führer is nowhere to be seen on our battlefield. No doubt, he is drawing up his ridiculous schemes from the safety of some bunker in Berlin.

"And you are here, my comrades in arms. It is my belief, *you* are the true Aryan race. So, join me."

Without hesitation, the soldiers, in their entirety, responded in kind.

. . .

"Now, get your asses inside and prime your tanks in readiness to move out. We leave in an hour!"

3:45 AM

Daniel squinted through the foggy windscreen. No matter how often he wiped the moisture off with his sleeve, the falling sleet immediately frosted it up again.

High speed mode for the Studebaker's wipers, resulted in no more than marginally clearing the muck and ice from the glass.

The execrable conditions meant the intrepid group failed to notice the US army jeep, König's men had shunted out of the way, or the three soldiers, slaughtered so callously.

His attention on the road directly ahead of him and barely visible under the truck's diminished headlights, Daniel's face paled when he was obliged to crank the steering wheel sharply to the right, braking hard to avoid colliding with the two ageing fire trucks whining and clunking through the darkness on their way to the inferno.

"Son of a bitch," he roared.

Daniel's unexpected manoeuvre sent the Studebaker skidding wildly towards the ditch. By the time he was able to bring the truck under control, the front wheels were suspended over the edge of the road.

Teetering on the brink of disaster, Jack pulled Evie to the gate of the truck, and ordered Paul to, "Get back here now, but whatever you do, move as carefully as possible."

When the Frenchman opened the passenger side door, the nose of the truck dipped downwards, prompting Jack to countermand his own directive. "Forget that, Paul. Stay where you are and everybody lean back."

With the door swinging on its hinges, the occupants in the vehicle followed Jack's command in unison.

The truck groaned as it rocked backwards. Its rear tyres settled once more on the slushy road.

"Sergeant Fisher, put this truck into reverse, and get us out of here."

Jack's order was a waste of breath. Daniel had already done so and was standing on the accelerator.

The Studebaker growled its disapproval of Daniel's abusive treatment, but the sergeant didn't care. The truck's tyres spun up globs of mud and sludge before finding a patch of ground solid enough to catch on, sending the two and a half ton behemoth to the middle of the road.

With no time to check on the condition of those in the truck bed, Daniel ground the gears until he found first. The vehicle careened forwards as he aimed the wheels at their destination.

The thud of angry feet on the wooden boards behind him was accompanied by a flood of obscenities regarding Daniel's woeful lack of driving skills.

Jack poked his head through the canvas, and concluded his rant with, "Never mind about following their tracks, just find us the biggest, goddamned building on this road."

Paul interjected before Daniel could reply.

"It will be coming up on your right, Major, in approximately one kilometre."

"How can you be so sure?"

"There are only a couple of structures still standing in Reims able to shelter a force of that size. Of those, there is only one on this road. Oh, and if you look closely, it appears to be occupied."

All eyes swung to the sprawling building, which loomed

up in front of them. Even the murky darkness failed to conceal its existence, illuminated by numerous lights burning within.

Jack jumped as the barrel of a Panzerfaust appeared next to him.

"Let me take the shot, Major," a feminine voice beseeched from somewhere down the weapon.

"And kill us in the process? Sorry, doll, no can do. Sergeant Fisher?"

"Aye, sir?"

"Bring us close to the entrance, and park. I have an idea."

Chapter Twenty-Three

4:00 AM

J ack had not dismissed Evie's appeal out of hand. There was merit in her suggestion to bring the building down on top of the Germans, but neither the Panzerfausts nor the M-9 rockets they carried were powerful enough to inflict more than superficial damage to the plant.

Best case scenario, they might be lucky enough to kill those not in their tanks, reducing further the contingent they were about to face.

Worst case, the tanks would protect the Germans, allowing them to plow their way through the inferior walls.

With the darkness their ally, the moment the Studebaker came to a halt, Jack tapped Daniel on the shoulder.

In a low tone, he ordered, "I need you and Paul back here immediately."

The two men struggled to climb from the truck's front seat through the opening in the canvas to the back. In the process, Daniel's boot hit the horn. All four froze, fearing the sharp blare would alert those in the building to their presence.

Hands grabbed the sergeant, yanking him unceremoniously into the tuck bed and tossing him onto the crates of waiting weapons.

Annoyed with himself, and feeling like an idiot, Daniel snatched the M1 rifle and its anti-tank rocket. Paul shook his head at the American and took the rocket launcher Evie had been holding.

"Gentlemen," Jack began, "I want the two of you to head to the left side of the main door. Evie and I will go to the right. Make sure to position yourselves at about a forty-five degree angle from the front. I don't want us accidentally blowing up each other."

Paul smothered a smile at the worthless caution. *Of course, immediately assume we are stupid enough to shoot at our friends,* he scoffed inwardly. *Then again when it came to American training, who could tell.*

Jack turned to Paul. "Monsieur Dufort, I know I have been disrespectful to you in the past and blackmailed you into this mess. For what it's worth, I apologise. I was wrong, you are a true patriot of France, and now I must beg from you, one more favour. Take that damned German popgun and consign the first thing that dares exit those doors to hell."

Jack threw a salute to the Frenchman, holding it until Paul reciprocated.

Both men slung their assigned weapons across their backs. Paul requested an M1 rifle of his own, as well as a satchel of M9 grenades, knowing the Panzerfaust was only good for a single shot. He was not about to be left out of the battle.

He had lost enough, and if this confrontation resulted in

him losing his life as well, it would surely mean he would be reunited with Henri in the afterlife.

Crawling across the squelchy ground on their stomachs, Paul and Daniel reached their assigned location whereupon, Paul rose to his knees and settled the German grenade launcher on his shoulder.

It was a procedure Evie mimicked from her side, lining up the sighting bead on the centre of the doors.

Daniel and Jack prepped the American rifles for the pending attack. Command had long since discovered the thicker armour of the newer German tanks were relatively impervious to these warheads but, according to Kristiansen, that was not what they were about to face.

The grenades would slice through the thinly clad French tanks like a hot knife through butter.

The quartet was barely ready when a voice bellowed, "Öffnen Sie schnell die Türen." (Quickly, open the doors!)

Two lanky soldiers, dressed in German Heer Panzer uniforms, appeared. They pushed open the doors to reveal the dazzle of headlights as the first tank began to exit the plant.

Paul took a breath in and held it.

As the Somua S35 trundled across the threshold, Paul fired the German rocket, hitting the tank beneath the gun turret. It detonated, blowing the cupola off the tank like the top of a fizzing soda bottle.

A sickening thud accompanied by a strangled shriek, implied the heavy lid had landed on someone behind the tank.

Evie's shot entered the tank through the driver's opened viewing hatch, detaching the man's head before detonating the shells, transforming the great wheeled bunker into an incendiary device.

All within, as well as any too close to the flaming bomb, were instantly reduced to ash.

Dropping the now useless weapons, Paul and Evie scooped up their M1s and prepared to annihilate anything else tempted to move.

They did not have to wait very long.

From inside the plant they heard one of the Germans bawl, "Gottverdammt, geh aus dem Weg." (Goddammit, get out of the way.)

Positive it was König, Jack tapped Evie on the shoulder to make sure she was ready in case their target decided to charge the fiery remains of the tank.

What happened next took those outside the plant completely by surprise.

The ground shook beneath them as two successive blasts ripped apart the wreckage blocking the doorway.

Shards of burning metal erupted into the night, causing the four to hit the ground to avoid being shredded into tiny pieces.

A tank barged over the debris. Its commander spotted the Studebaker parked at the boundary of the plant's lighting. He barked an order and the tank swerved to face the truck head-on.

A second instruction brought a moment of silence, followed by the thunder of the S-35's gun. The percussion and fire which followed the projectile as it exited the cannon, meant the Germans had upgraded the old tanks from their original forty-seven millimetre peashooter to something significantly more powerful.

That part of the battle was over almost before it began. The truck and its cargo of weapons lit up the darkness as it was catapulted off the ground. Smashing back to earth, the impact ejected the grenades in the rear in every direction.

In the confusion, an unknown number of tanks managed to escape onto the field, although not without casualties. Panzerfaust rockets slammed into the sides of a couple of S-35s before they could manoeuvre out of the way.

One of the tanks inside the plant rammed a wall in an effort to escape. Unwittingly, the driver, in his zeal, ruptured the natural gas line once used by the plant to power the grain milling machinery.

The ensuing conflagration levelled the building onto anything and anyone who remained within.

Evie glanced at Jack, observing caustically, "See, we could have saved the poor truck if you had allowed me to shoot the building."

Jack was readying himself when the glare of searchlights flooded the complex from the ridge above them.

Hurriedly, Evie reloaded her M1, expecting this to be some sort of German counterstrike.

The American major smiled and shook his head. He had been around tanks enough to recognise the distinct rumbling of M4 Shermans entering the conflict.

Pointing to the red, white, and blue flag fluttering above the turret of the lead tank, he yelled, "Looks like Leclerc is on time for once!"

Jack and Evie watched the American provided tanks surge through the mass of French S-35's, but it was not a cakewalk for Leclerc's men, either.

Even though the Shermans' armoured hulls held the advantage, both opponents carried the same main cannon. Each pounded the other's tanks, inflicting heavy damage, igniting horrendous fires within their cabins, arbitrarily claiming the lives of their soldiers. The only true advantage Leclerc had over König was in sheer numbers of tanks.

Jack spotted one of König's S-35's bearing down on them, in an apparent attempt to flee the destruction. Angling his M1 to fire on it, he was met by a short barrage from the tank's Reibel machine gun.

The first shot caught him in his left shoulder, throwing him sideways. It left him vulnerable to the second bullet, which penetrated his lung, and exited through his back, a hair's breadth from his spine.

Seeing Jack fall, Evie grabbed him by the scruff of his collar, dragging him into a crater left by an errant Panzer-faust rocket.

Pressing her body tightly to Jack's, Evie waited for them to be crushed to death.

Unsure whether he could hear her over the din, the words spilled over anyway, "Do not even *think* about dying, Jack Donovon. I refuse to let another man leave me... even if it is *you*."

Evie felt the ground tremble as the S-35 rolled above them. Believing this was their end, she clutched Jack. All light and sound vanished, save the roar of the engine.

Slowly, rays of the complex's lights began to bleed into the muddy divot. Cautiously, Evie turned her head to see the rear of the solid, black mass pass over them.

Not bothering to calculate the odds of their survival, Evie grabbed Jack's loaded M1.

Aiming the best she could, she pulled the trigger.

König could only see the open field before him. He was not fool enough to believe *one* tank would reach Paris... let alone create the desired chaos and destruction even if, perchance, it could.

I am sorry, mein Führer, if I have to choose between your madness and my life... I would rather see the sunrise.

It was not to be.

Evie's grenade struck the S-35's chassis, burrowing its way into the fuel tank. The smoke and fire which consumed the interior torched the lining of König's lungs before the ensuing explosion claimed his life.

Evie did not waste time watching the demise of the tank. Certain Jack was at death's door she had to prevent him from crossing over. Risking frostbite, she removed her coat and covered Jack, applying pressure where she could.

She looked up at the sound of footfalls.

"Evie," Paul exhorted. "Are you hurt?"

"Non, Paul, but I fear Jack is mortally wounded."

A voice she did not recognise chimed in, "Perhaps, I could be of assistance?"

In the glare of a Sherman searchlight, Evie made out the uniform of an officer of the Free French Army, standing next to his tank.

"Please, I beg you, Monsieur, please save this man."

The officer instructed his radioman, "Caporal Vernier, contact HQ and have them dispatch a helicopter to our location immediately."

"Oui, Général Leclerc, right away."

Satisfied the man would carry out his order, Leclerc joined Evie in the hole.

"Madame, I am by no means a surgeon, but allow me to see what aid I can provide for him.

Chapter Twenty-Four

Central Sector
Ardennes Forest
5:30 AM

Private Jefferson Davis Scott, of the 106th Infantry Division, could not feel his legs. He repeated his prayer to the good Lord to transfer him back to Fort Jackson in South Carolina if only for a day to warm up.

Regrettably, the good Lord was otherwise occupied, and Scott had been freezing his ass off, for hours, exposed to the frigid German winter, convinced his northern-born sergeant was intent on inducing hypothermia in the Alabama native.

Perched high in a tree, since three in the morning, on a couple of boards his superior had generously described as a sniper's platform, Scott had finally run out of cuss words to direct at the man who had ordered him up here.

Checking his watch, Scott took another look through his binoculars to the east of his position… seeing zilch.

"Dagnabbit, Sarge," Scott groused into the early morning, "There ain't nothing out here, 'ceptin' trees and snow. Not even Hitler would be crazy enough to wander around in this mess."

And that was when he heard it.

The crunch of a tall tree falling beneath heavy machinery.

"Jesus Christ," he muttered. "Who would be stupid enough to log out here in a snow storm." The only logical conclusion because HQ had assured them, the Germans were nowhere near.

Without further warning, the Ardennes Forest came alive with the same recurring sound... but the sound was not stationary... it was advancing directly towards him.

Peering through his binoculars, Scott spotted the first of the Panzer tanks. As he reached for his walkie talkie, the binoculars tumbled from the tree.

"Is anybody there?" Scott screamed into the radio. "Pick up for the love of God! The entire German army is coming for breakfast! Anybody... pick—"

With no time to climb down from the tree, Scott jumped out, just as his position was bulldozed by the lead tank. The snow cushioned his fall, leaving him with a broken leg, but did nothing to protect him from being crushed by the Panzer onslaught which lumbered over him.

Reims, France
5:30 AM

Evie pressed her lips together to keep them from quivering as she watched the Sikorsky R-6 rise slowly from the ground, with Jack strapped to an external stretcher.

It was 115 kilometres to the nearest field hospital in Ravenel and, even if he survived the hazards of flying on one of those new American contraptions, especially with the weather closing in, she worried he would die on the operating table.

Leclerc had done an admirable job of stemming Jack's bleeding but, regrettably, the bullet had punctured his lung.

It had taken guidance over the radio from a doctor at the 21st General Hospital to perform a chest tube insertion.

Time being of the essence, Leclerc made do with what was available and used a convenient piece of thin rubber hose, Vernier had found in the tank, to inflate Jack's lung.

After several heart-stopping minutes, the French general managed to save Jack's life or, at least, buy sufficient time to get him to an operating theatre.

While this drama was unfolding, Caporal Vernier had been advised in no uncertain terms that, owing to the deteriorating weather, all helicopters were grounded.

Leclerc threatened military courts-martial, and declared heads would roll, if one was not dispatched to his location without delay to retrieve the American.

Evie had not yet thanked the general for his heroic deeds.

As the helicopter reached altitude and sped toward the northwest, she sensed Leclerc alongside her.

"Fear not, ma chéri," Leclerc said, endeavouring to cheer the woman. "Your man is—"

"I beg your pardon, mon Général, you are mistaken. Major Donovon and I are not in a personal relationship. He is simply a member of my resistance cell. I have no more concern for him than I would if it was one of those two—"

Evie waved her hand at Daniel and Paul, whose surprised expressions made her realise she had misunderstood the general's inference and, by jumping to conclusions, merely confirmed what she had tried to refute.

Caporal Vernier scrambling out of the turret alleviated the awkwardness of the situation.

"Mon Général. Headquarters to speak with you."

Climbing aboard, Leclerc took the mike and headset from the man. "Leclerc, here. Oui, the situation in Reims has been quelled. I assume de Gaulle will ensure the authorities here will be placated with some inane explan…"

He broke off mid-word, and blanched as he listened to the person on the other end of the radio.

"Are you sure the information is correct?" Leclerc snapped. "This would not be the first time American reconnaissance got their information wrong."

Once again, he listened intently.

"Oui, I understand. My men and I will head there without delay."

Returning the equipment to the caporal, Leclerc mumbled something as Vernier disappeared down the hatch, then leant over the rim to order, "Passez le mot. Préparez-vous à déménager." (Pass the word. Prepare to move out.")

Leclerc's tank fired up and, as the general was poised to climb inside, Daniel spoke, "General Leclerc, what about us? Where does HQ want us to go to be debriefed?"

"Nowhere, Sergeant. As far as anyone in Allied Command is concerned, this never happened."

"But, General, surely the French want to know what happened to their—"

"Sergeant, listen to me very closely. None of us… neither you nor I, and especially not the Germans… were ever in Reims. No one in Paris, London, or Washington wants to take credit for this debacle.

"If I hear anything to the contrary, I will see to it you are brought up on charges of sedition. Do you understand?

"Now, if you will excuse me, hell just ploughed through the Allied lines in the Ardennes Forest."

Valentin Submarine Pens
Bridge of Unterseeboot 3523
Rekum, Germany
5:30 AM

Kapitänleutnant Karl Grimm checked his pocket watch for the umpteenth time. It was already oh-five-thirty and the submarine was still being loaded with passengers and their personal belongings.

The U-3523's skipper had cut his teeth as a machinist's mate aboard the Kaiser's U-boat fleet during the Great War. His experience during those early days of hunting with the German Wolf Pack had instilled within Grimm the importance of following a schedule to the second.

The knowledge his ship was to be launched during low tide was preposterous enough, but to do so with an added retinue and unnecessary cargo made him consider scuttling the boat before the British did it for them.

"Herr Bormann," Grimm demanded the immediate attention of the Gestapo officer taking up space on the former's bridge. "It is of utmost importance that we get underway, this instant. Tell your people to finish whatever it is they are stowing on my boat and make sure your damned doctor has disembarked."

Looking at the time and the tide charts, he grunted, "I fail to understand why my ship's doctor could not attend to the needs of your *passengers?*"

"Patience, mein Kapitän," Martin Bormann's patronising tone, left Grimm clenching his fists so he didn't punch the supercilious twerp.

"Not even you would wish to rush Dr. Mengele and his surgical skills. The level he achieved while practicing in his laboratories, we set up in the concentration camps, has advanced the field of facial reconstruction far beyond anything the Americans or the British could imagine.

"I assure you, Dr Mengele has prepared your guest and his woman for the trip and will be departing shortly." Bormann chuckled at seeing his plan come to fruition. "The transformation wrought by the doctor is so remarkable, even the couple in question will not recognise themselves."

"I do not care what madness you and the party have dreamt up. The sooner that Death Dealer is off my ship the better," Grimm retorted.

"Fear not, Kapitän. Do you want me to ask the good doctor to leave you something to ease your nerves?"

"I would rather slit my own throat than take any drugs he is peddling."

A voice crackled on the submarine's intercom, "Kapitän Grimm, the doctor has escorted Dr. Mengele from the ship."

"It is about time," Grimm scowled.

Paying no heed to the captain's discontent, Bormann clapped his hands in satisfaction. "Everything is going as planned. Dr. Mengele will be delivered safely to our contacts at the Vatican. I anticipate the cardinals will have him in Buenos Aires to meet us at the docks."

"It does not hurt that the head of the Catholic Church is a hidden German asset," Grimm scoffed, checking his watch for a final time. "Now, Herr Bormann, if you would kindly vacate my bridge, we can still launch while there is enough water in the channel to carry us out to the North Sea."

As Bormann prepared to step through the exit into the adjoining hallway, Grimm was overcome with curiosity as to the future of Germany.

"If our guest is sedated, who is left in Berlin to bring this catastrophic loss of life to a suitable conclusion?"

Bormann's reply dripped with sarcasm, "The same dawdling

drug addict who has been handing out medals for the past six months. If the country is adamant in their belief, he is indeed Adolph Hitler, then they deserve the fate which awaits them.

On his way out, Bormann felt the need to have the last word. "Make sure to notify me when we reach the open sea."

A cafe in Reims
6:10 AM

Evie, Paul, and Daniel trudged through the driving snow to the town's centre. Fortunately, they came across a cordial shop owner who had come to work early in hopes of serving the hordes who had been scurrying about Reims looking for fires and Germans.

He ushered them inside, to a corner table. He had dealt with enough questionable people during the occupation to ensure none had their backs to the door. It was simply a sixth sense.

Providing them with a pot of steaming coffee... *actual coffee*... and three cups, he smiled and left them with a reminder that if they wanted anything else, the kitchen would open in about half an hour.

Evie poured the coffee for everyone. Neither man moved until she finished.

Setting down the pot, Evie looked at her cup as the dark liquid settled. At last, she lifted it and, in a soft voice, toasted her companions.

"To us, gentlemen. Paris will never know what we did for her."

She took a sip and heard Paul add, "And to Henri. Even though he despised war, he sacrificed himself all the same."

Daniel smiled and replied, "Hear, hear! And to Jack Donovon for knowing what he was talking about."

A hush fell over the table.

It was Paul who reassured Evie. "Genevieve, in the short time since we met, I have come to appreciate Major Donovon's stubborn perseverance. I have faith he will recover."

Evie did not respond. She drank her coffee and listened to the others discussing their return to Paris.

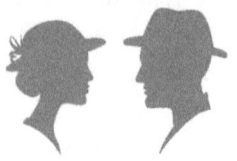

Chapter Twenty-Five

21st General Hospital
Ravenel, France
27th December 1944

During the previous ten days, there had been talk of evacuating the hospital complex for fear the German advance would put it on the wrong side of the battlefront.

On the previous day, some of its buildings were strafed by enemy planes and the grounds were struck by a bomb. Fortunately, no one was injured and the damage slight.

Jack Donovon had played only witness to the action from the confines of his hospital bed.

The closest he came to battle was a furious confrontation with the head nurse about staying put. *She* had threatened to strap him to his mattress if he tried to move.

Fed up, Jack resigned himself to recuperating, and scouring reports about the incursion of thirty divisions of tanks which was being referred to, euphemistically, as the Battle of the Bulge.

Discarding the dossiers, Jack brooded over what he had just read.

"Ain't that cute? Wonder which bright spark came up with *that* description? Sounds more like a weight loss program than a fight to the death."

His irritation was exacerbated by what was missing from the dispatches. There was no mention of the Reims incident. While it did not come as a shock that the story was not released in its entirety, he *had* hoped Allied Command would revoke their accusations that he had lost his mind.

Maybe I have for thinking anybody would admit to the monumental fuck up, Jack ruminated as he closed his eyes. His temples were throbbing... a nap might be just the ticket.

"Nurse?"

At the sound of a familiar voice, Jack cracked open one eye.

"I am looking for Major Jack Donovon."

"Bed twenty-six, miss. But I think he is asle—"

"Evie," Jack hailed her, and sat up.

"Thank you, nurse. I believe I have located him.

"I'm happy somebody is here to distract him." The nurse sighed in exasperation. "Do us all a favour and take him with you when you leave."

Evie sent the nurse an understanding smile, and walked along the ward to Jack's bed. She repositioned the chair until it was next to him and sat down.

"Is there anywhere you are welcome, Major Donovon?"

"I don't think the welcomes are the problem, Evie. I reckon it's more like the extended stays."

Canting her head, she agreed, "That much is true."

Evie was not in the mood for small talk. She had not seen Jack for nearly two weeks, and the US army had resisted her persistent requests to visit him.

It had taken some arm twisting by her new found friend in the form of a French general to be granted permission.

Now, she was here, she was hesitant to broach the question she had traveled a hundred kilometres to ask, so blurted out, "What are your plans when they release you?"

Jack shrugged. "I guess I'll head back to my office in Paris and await my next orders. I'm sure you and I can come up with something to keep us occupied until they arrive. Perhaps you could show me around—"

Evie's face collapsed into a frown.

By the change in her expression, Jack realised his answer was not the one she wanted to hear.

Desperate to change the subject, Evie let slip, "Jack, you no longer have an office in Le Meurice. Philippe said—"

Merde… Evie berated herself internally, today was probably *not* the best time to tell him, he was still recovering, but it was too late to retract her statement.

The news about his office took second place to Evie's casual mention of another man's name. Jack's brow arched… *who the hell was Philippe?* "Philippe?" He fought to sound nothing more than mildly interested, shocked by the wave of envy which swamped him.

Attuned to the slightest change in Jack's demeanour, Evie picked up on his resentful tone and, while acknowledging it was pointless trying to reason with him, gave it a shot.

Outwardly calm, she elaborated, "Oui, Général Leclerc. Despite his stalwart efforts to thwart the sustained campaign by the Germans to stymie the Allied advance into the Fatherland, he saw fit to take the time to assist me in certain… delicate matters."

"How very thoughtful of him. Taking up with generals now are you?" Jack bit out sarcastically. He did not mean to sound like a jealous lover but, for the life of him, could not curb his tongue.

In fact, the emotion itself was foreign to him. He had never experienced it with any woman until Evie.

It confused him further because... save the night they danced... their relationship had been strictly business, studiously ignoring the uproarious laughter at the back of his head at his naïveté.

"Say what you will, Major Donovon, but he convinced de Gaulle to rescind his banishment of Paul and me."

"I will make sure to thank him when I see him. Did he happen to mention why *I* have been displaced?"

"Oui, Major, because you are an imbecile," Evie huffed. "The moment de Gaulle heard you were shot, *Phillippe...*"

Just hearing Evie say Leclerc's name was like a knife to Jack's heart.

"...said the general was on the phone to Roosevelt insisting you be relieved of duty for insubordination. Evidently, the continuing goodwill between our two countries depends on you being removed from France permanently."

Her words cut Jack deeply. He pondered his next question, carefully.

"Are... are you planning to stay in Paris then?"

Even had Evie *not* deciphered Jack's bewilderment regarding their burgeoning relationship... or apparent lack thereof... she was equally baffled, unaware that her grief at losing something which had barely begun, echoed Jack's.

Without answering, she rose from the chair, stroked her gloved hand against his cheek, and turned to leave, only to stop at his....

"Evie? What are you going to do?"

She kept her face averted, unwilling for him to see her weep. "Jack, for all intents and purposes, the war is over, and we are both adult enough to know that wartime romances end at the signing of the peace treaty. We hardly got to know each other in the first place.

"I intend to accept General de Gaulle's offer, and will be accompanying Paul and Daniel to America. Au revoir, Jack. May your life be everything you could wish for."

Pressing her trembling lips together, Evie hurried from the ward.

Epilogue

Calais, France
19th February 1945
9:00 AM

I n the cool grey light of the winter's morning, Evie stood on the docks with Paul and Daniel, waiting to board their respective ships.

Originally, the three believed they would be traveling together but, for some reason — which no one thought pertinent to disclose — that was not the case.

Daniel was required to sail aboard a troop carrier heading for Boston. Paul had been accorded a berth on a Liberty vessel transporting refugees to Norfolk, Virginia, while Evie was granted passage on a hospital ship bound for New York.

"Evie," Daniel entreated excitedly when the horn on his ship summoned its soldiers to begin embarking, "since you'll be in the Big Apple too, make sure to look me up so we can arrange to meet in Times Square for the holidays."

Even though Evie knew it would never come to fruition, she grinned at Daniel as he was jostled by those wanting to go home. "That sounds wonderful, Sergeant Fisher."

She could not put her finger on *why* she knew, it was just a feeling.

Maybe because people hate the finality of saying goodbye.

Halfway up the gangway, Daniel hollered, "You come too, Paul."

Paul's intuition mirrored Evie's, but he nodded and waved an acknowledgment to Daniel before facing Evie.

"Did you bid Claude au revoir?"

"Oui, I spent yesterday afternoon at his grave," Evie mustered up a melancholy smile. "If anything positive can be said about the Germans, it is that their bureaucracy in identifying and burying the dead is meticulous."

Her vague attempt at injecting a hint of humour, scarcely elicited the obligatory grin from Paul.

Pursing her lips at her failure to lighten the mood, she added, "I did try to explain to him why I could not stay in France, why I had to leave him behind. I pray he was watching from Heaven and understood."

"I have no doubt he was." Paul's obvious sincerity eased Evie's lingering sense of guilt. He paused for a moment. "I wish I had met the man, Evie."

"I am sure Claude would have found favour with you, Paul, though he might have had a problem with Henri's capitalistic views."

"I'll wager the two are arguing economics as we speak."

They shared a chuckle.

Paul glanced at his watch.

"Mon pote, it is time for me to bid you adieu. My ship is set to depart within the hour, and I have yet to locate its berth."

Evie brushed a kiss to his cheek, and whispered softly in his ear, "Be safe in America, my friend."

Paul bowed with typical French gallantry...

"You as well, my dear Madame Rousseau."

...then vanished into the throng.

Alone, Evie picked up her suitcase. She scanned the docks for the final time and, despite knowing the one person she wanted to see was not there, hope died hard. She had not spoken to Jack since that disastrous day at the hospital.

Inhaling a lungful of French air, something she would never smell again, Evie made her way to the hospital ship's gangway.

Before she had set foot on the plank, a burly hand touched her shoulder, taking Evie by surprise. Without looking behind, her heart began to flutter.

About to spin around and slap the arrogant American's face for making her believe he would let her go, her heart shattered when an unfamiliar, nasal-sounding voice, addressed her in French.

"Are you Genevieve Rousseau?"

Turning to answer, Evie recalled how often she had been asked that question, and the countless times it had been necessary to deny it.

Today was not going to be one of them.

She replied sharply, "Oui, I am Genevieve Rousseau and, as you can see, I am about to depart for New York. If you have anything to say, please make it quick."

The soldier stood with his hands clasped behind his back. Next to him, a second soldier who looked no less formidable.

The first soldier answered flatly, "Madame Rousseau, we have been ordered to prevent you from boarding this ship. Your travel plans have been rescinded and I am to confiscate your papers."

Evie was furious. "On whose orders? My papers were signed by none other than Charles de Gaulle. Now, if you will excuse me, I have no time for this foolishness."

She pivoted on her heel preparing to ascend the gangway, but once again the meaty hand landed on her shoulder.

"Madame Rousseau, we have orders to detain you physically, if necessary."

"And that is why there are two of you? Because I represent too much of a danger for one large French soldier?"

"We were shown your dossier, Madame," the soldier defended diffidently.

Shoving between the duo, Evie exhorted, "Fine, take me to General Leclerc. I am sure he is involved in this somehow. I will see both of you reduced to guard duty for the rest of your miserable lives."

The soldiers shared a resigned glance before catching up to her, one on either side.

The men escorted Evie in silence, leading her off the dock and to an area set aside for vehicles.

There, like a huge black beetle, sat the same brash, two-door Peugeot 402 Eclipse she had been coerced into, that fateful night when she met Major Jackson Donovon — scant weeks yet a lifetime ago.

The same urge to shoot the man behind the wheel and flee, possessed her, but she did not have her pistol, and the two soldiers shovelling her into the passenger seat, while outwardly indifferent to her protests, looked very fit.

I don't fancy being tackled to the ground by either of those gorillas, or shot in the back by one of them, she mused cynically.

The car door slammed shut. Evie slumped in her seat, her arms folded.

Glaring through the windscreen, she snapped, "Can I assume, besides auto theft, you have added kidnapping to your repertoire of legally sanctioned crimes? Oh wait... you already did that to Daniel, Paul, and Henri."

"Evie please, I beg you, please allow me to speak," Jack implored.

"Major Donovan, you made your opinion of me clear at the hospital ward. Permit me to take my leave while there remains a slim possibility I can board my ship and get the hell away from you."

Evie jiggled the Peugeot's door handle, but Jack reached over and grasped her wrist before she could get it unlocked. His grip did not hurt, but was tight enough to compel her to face him at last.

At which, Evie punched him in the jaw.

Through hot tears, she hiccuped, "Why could you not just allow me to go? Do you know how much pain I have been in since you were shot in Reims... and then to have you accuse me of sleeping with General—"

"Please, Evie, I have been a confused mess since the night I met you. No woman has ever ensnared me, bewitched me, the way you have. I know, I don't deserve your forgiveness. Madame Leclerc all but told me that when I went to the general's residence."

Infuriated, Evie chose to ignore the elated frisson upon hearing she had she ensnared and bewitched him. "Oh, please tell me you were not crazy enough to confront Phillippe at his house?"

"I figured if I was about to lose you to a superior officer, I had the right to demand satisfaction."

"For God's sake, Jack, this is 1945, not 1745."

Jack parried, "Well, it never got that far, anyway. By the time Thérèse intervene—"

"*Thérèse?*" Evie's tone rose a notch.

"The venerable Madame Leclerc." Jack rubbed his chin, ruefully. "By the way, I would suggest you forgo introducing yourself to her, she can really pack a wallop if she's crossed. In fact, I would recommend you avoid her at all costs. You are not on her most favourite list."

"You truly are an idiot." Evie shook her head, her outrage deflating marginally.

Jack shrugged unrepentantly. "At least when I explained the situation to the missus, she redirected her temper at her husband. He's claiming the black eye he is sporting as a battle injury. Even going so far as to put himself in for a battle medal. Witnessing his wife land the punch also helped me to procure your escorts."

"And, now you can add extortion… never mind… that's another threshold you crossed a long time ago."

While enlightening, this discussion was not getting them anywhere. They were skirting around the point.

"Tell me what it is you want, Major Donovon?" Evie didn't bother to mask her exasperation.

"I want *you*, Genevieve Rousseau. If I could take back the last month and a half, I would. I need you in my life… beside me… through thick and thin."

"As cannon fodder? No thank you, I'll pass," Evie retorted.

"No," Jack promised. "There will be no more tanks. I can assure you of that... almost," he felt he ought to qualify.

Evie tilted her head. "Is that invitation supposed to make me want to shed my knickers for you?"

Jack swallowed hard, aware... in order to win Evie... he had to confess his true feelings for the first time in his life.

His mouth went dry, as he opened his heart. "No, well... yes... but more importantly, Evie Rousseau, I love you. I promise to protect you every day of my life, no matter the circumstances, and to make sure your knickers are shed with passionate abandon, every night."

Evie gaped at him, momentarily speechless. Well, now he had gone and professed what she wanted to hear when she visited him in the hospital. A warm tingle began to undulate down her spine, but she was not *quite* ready to relent.

Maintaining her equanimity with effort, she asked, "What am I going to do with you, Jack Donovon?"

"Whatever you like." He sent her a wicked grin, and the seductive timbre of his voice intensified the gentle glissade into delicious shivers which rippled right through Evie, all the way to her toes... which she swore curled in the brand new traveling shoes.

He took her hand and stared into her eyes. "Stay with me forever... and come with me to Buenos Aires. It would make the perfect honeymoon destination."

"Honeymoon? Wait, Jack, are you asking me to marry..." Evie arched an eyebrow, "...hold it, Mister, are you after that submarine?"

"Well, yeah, now you mention it, there *was* a report of a German U-boat surfacing off the Argentinian coast a week or so ago. Washington organised two plane tickets to fly down there and check it out. Buenos Aires has plenty of beautiful chapels, too. Please come with me," he wheedled.

Knowing this was one battle she would lose, Evie capitulated with a single stipulation. "Only if you feed me. You still owe me lunch, and I'm starving."

Jack leant over to envelop her in his embrace.

With uncharacteristic shyness, Evie raised her face to his.

Their kiss, long and deep with no hesitation or reservation, held the promise of forever.

Jack lifted his head. "I know a little cafe which serves incredible coffee."

"Jack Donovon, don't you dare take me to the Café la Fête, or I'll hit you with that famous coffee's pot."

"It's a bit early for lunch so, how about a full breakfast on the *Dame de Fer*? For the sake of my safety." Jack chuckled.

"Sounds perfect." Evie sank into her seat, as Jack fired up the Peugeot.

A weight rolled off Evie's shoulders. Her war might be over but, imagining the adventures life had in store, she suspected the years ahead would be anything but peaceful!

But that was in the future.

Beignets on the deck of the Eiffel Tower came first.

About the Author

Rori Bleu

With a smattering of riverboat pirates and royalty in her heritage, Rori Bleu's childhood reflected her past.
An interest in fairy tales, myth and legend were as important as spirited discussions around politics and current affairs — although some might argue they are one and the same!

A fascination, sparked by listening to Grimm's Fairy Tales at her grandmother's knee, not only encouraged Rori's passion for reading, but also steered her into the world of RPG's. What began as a fun pastime, soon evolved into the creation of fantastical worlds, but Rori never lost her love of politics going on to specialise in Governmental History and Historical Research.

Naturally this means her stories are steeped in historical accuracy and real-life intrigue. While Rori's love of a happily ever after means her preferred genre is romance, don't be surprised if you discover an occasional detour into historical fiction, thrillers, horror and fantasy.

To find more of Rori's books… click the link
https://linktr.ee/roribleu

About the Author
Rosie Chapel

Rosie Chapel lives in Perth, Australia with her hubby and three furkids. When not writing, she loves catching up with friends, burying herself in a book (or three), discovering the wonders of Western Australia, or — and the best — a quiet evening at home with her husband, enjoying a glass of wine and a movie.

Website: www.rosiechapel.com

Also by Rori Bleu

Pineapple Meringue

Imprisoned Hearts

Port of London

Dani's Masquerade

Black Tulips

Ajei's Destiny

Porta Aeternum

Syn *with Matthew Forester*

Echoes and Illusions *with Rosie Chapel*

Also by Rosie Chapel

Rescuing Her Knight

Elusive Hearts - *An Unexpected Romance*: Book One

His Fiery Hoyden

A Regency Duet

A Regency Christmas Double

Fate is Curious

A Christmas Prayer *with Ashlee Shades*

The Lady's Wager

Winning Emma

A Love Impossible

Unravelling Roana

Love Kindled

Fairy Tale Romance

Chasing Bluebells

Contemporary Romances

Of Ruins and Romance

All At Once It's You

Cobweb Dreams

Just One Step

His Heart's Second Sigh

Dystopian Romance

Echoes & Illusions *with Rori Bleu*